A Promise to Catie

A Promise to Catie

A Novel
by
Judd Holt

University of North Texas Press
Denton, Texas

10 9 8 7 6 5 4 3 2 1

The paper used in this book meets the minimum requirements
of the American National Standard for Permanence of Paper
for Printed Library Materials, Z39.48.1984. Binding materials
have been chosen for durability.

Library of Congress Cataloging-in-Publication Data

Holt, Judd. 1941—
A promise to Catie / Judd Holt.
p.   cm.
ISBN 0-929398-41-6
I. Title.
PS3558.0398P7   1992
813'. 54—dc20

92-9905
CIP

To Suzy, Josh, Judd, and Jonathan

PART ONE

Clear Creek

He who bends to himself a Joy
Does the wingèd life destroy;
But he who kisses the Joy as it flies
Lives in Eternity's sunrise.

"Eternity" William Blake

Star-light, star-bright
First star I see tonight;
I wish I may, I wish I might,
Get the wish I wish tonight.

Unknown

1955

Maybe things weren't really better then. I was just younger.

Dwight David Eisenhower was President, and even though we had fought another war since 1945, World War II was still "The War," and events were always referenced by it. "Before the war." "During the war." "After the war." In 1955 a kid made only 60 to 90 cents an hour at summer or part-time work, but an hour's work would buy most of his necessities of life. I remember that admission to movies was 20 cents; popcorn, a dime; hamburgers, a quarter; french fries, 15 cents; shakes, a quarter; and gasoline 20 cents a gallon. A comic book cost a dime and paperback books were only a quarter.

In 1955 *Marty* won the Academy Award for best picture, and *East of Eden* and *Oklahoma* were other favorites that year. Those were the days when a new movie came to the theater every two or three days, and I saw as many of them as I could.

Back then, few people in Texas had air-conditioned homes. So, even if things were quieter in those days, you always heard the sounds of the city or of the country through the open windows. The noise couldn't be shut out as it can today. Nor could the dust. Back then the United States Supreme Court had recently decided *Brown vs. The Board of Education* and the segregation of black and white children in the schools was presumably at an end. I turned fourteen that year and pretty well completed my climb into puberty, an event of great significance only to me. On second thought, it probably had some importance for my parents, also. They said the new hormones in me bounced around like a steel ball careening forever in a pinball machine.

1955 and the following year were the ones I will always remember more vividly than any other years of my life. You will understand why after you read this account. What happened to me during those years was not ordinary by anyone's standards. In fact, it was so unbelievable, I've told only one person, and she is long since dead. I've been married twenty-three years and not even my wife has heard what I'm about to tell, though if she did, she probably would just smile, shake her head, and think I was only pulling her leg again. Possibly there was a time when a few of my adolescent friends and perhaps my little sister had an idea that something strange was happening to me. Most likely, however, they thought the strangeness was only a part of my personality and not the result of some unknown, outside force preying on me. Whatever their suspicions might have been then, the intervening years have caused those friends to relegate whatever thoughts they might have had about my behavior to some back shelf of their brains. There, the memories can't be recaptured except as vague, dreamlike events where what really happened cannot be distinguished from what did not happen. My sister, Beth, the only person who should remember what occurred, has not, for many years, even alluded to that long-ago time.

Now, however, almost thirty-seven years have passed since those days, and even though very few people will believe me, it's time for me to relate what happened.

In January 1955, I was thirteen and our family was moving from Dallas to an old farmhouse out in the country, north of the small college town of Oakpoint, Texas.

Dad was driving and talking in an exuberant voice, which was not unusual for him. Mother, seated beside him, had been silent since we passed the Dallas city limits. Her quietness was unusual. My sister Beth and I were in the back seat, our moods somewhere between those of our parents.

"It won't be long now," Dad said. Without waiting for a response he continued, "Just look at that view." He was serious. Ahead of us was a long, narrow highway with prairie on either side as far as I could see. Prairie and sky, their endlessness broken only by telephone lines, a few leafless mesquites in the pastures and winter brown small trees and brush along the fence lines. "Now this is what I call country," Dad exclaimed, waving one hand about.

Mother, who had not adjusted to the idea of moving from Dallas, kept her eyes on the road ahead, like she was in a trance. I looked at Beth, who was ten, and she stared at me with a what-in-the-world-are-we-doing-here look. I answered her look by scrunching my shoulders in a "beats me" manner, then I stuck my hand out the window and moved it up with the wind against my palm pretending to go over the top of a telephone pole, then down to the ground, then over the next pole until Dad told me to shut the window.

"Where are the trees?" Beth asked Dad in a sarcastic way.

As if he were surveying the most magnificent ranch in the world, he answered, "Oh, they're here. Just wait. A couple of miles up there's a ridge, and a large creek flows beneath it. They call it Clear Creek. It's covered with trees that follow it from wherever it comes from to wherever it goes." Dad could be dramatic.

Beth leaned over to me and whispered, "I hope they're bigger than those pitiful ones out there."

"I think that's the movers," Mother finally spoke as she pointed to a cloud of dust that moved slowly off to the left ahead of us. We soon turned off the pavement onto gravel and followed our worldly possessions down the bleak road. When we reached our new home, the moving van turned into the driveway and disappeared behind the far side of the house. Dad parked in front, and he, Mother, and Beth walked back to watch the movers. I stood by the car, alone, facing the front door across the yard. The straw-like dead grass of the lawn met the gravel of the road just beneath my feet. On one side of the house was a barbed wire fence, the posts made from small, crooked trees. Far back and to the left of the house was an out-of-commission windmill with a broken, staggering look like an old street-corner beggar. A few scrubby, bare shrubs stood in front of the porch, and one large tree, its biggest limbs split off by lightning, wind, or maybe just old age, interrupted the bareness of the yard. A broken swing, unused for many years, hung from the largest remaining branch. I stared at the old house for a few seconds. Something was wrong. I closed my eyes a second or two, squeezing them tightly then blinking three or four times before opening them again.

I had a strange sensation the house was staring back at me.

The house my mother and dad purchased to satisfy my dad's dream of living in the country was a white frame home built, as nearly as I've been able to find out, between 1900 and 1910. The house was L-shaped. The front part was two-story, and the part that formed the top of the L was one-story. A wide porch stretched across the front. My bedroom was a large room on the second floor at the back of the front wing of the house. From its windows, I could look north toward several grassy hills that dropped rather sharply on their far side to the stream named Clear Creek. Beneath my windows was a ragged, disheveled garden. To my left was the north wing of the house which protected the garden from the heat of the afternoon Texas sun which was capable of burning anything with color to a crisp, particularly in August and early September, before the first cool northers would blow in and rescue us from the dog days of summer.

The garden was a flower garden like some of the wealthy people in Dallas had. At its center was a fountain. Surrounding the fountain were benches and stepping stones and several beds with small trees and space for flowers and ground covers. The area was partially shaded by three native Texas trees, two hackberries and a crepe myrtle. I remember the garden mostly as a place where strange exchanges took place.

You can't make a judgment on changes in your life until the novelty of a new situation has worn off. There are always a few weeks when the excitement of the change either causes you to imagine you've found the promised land or at least masks the reality that what you now have is no better or may be even inferior to what you had before. This was true for me. For a short period after we moved into the country house, I didn't miss Dallas. The countryside had enough variety and novelty to keep me interested and occupied, and just about the time when I would have begun to really miss my old neighborhood and friends, something occurred which took Dallas out of my mind completely.

It began one school night, a Thursday, a couple of months after we had moved into the farm house. While my parents and my sister had gone to an open house at Beth's school, I had stayed at home. Although I had never been alone in the house after dark, I don't remember having any particular fear of being by myself. Staying alone had never bothered me when we lived in Dallas, and it didn't bother me in an isolated house, either.

That late March night was unseasonably warm and humid. I settled down in the kitchen and watched *Dragnet*. The next program was boring, so I flipped off the TV, picked up a book, and went to the living room to read. The name of the book was *The Big Eye*. It was a science fiction story about a planet or some other type of world heading toward an inevitable collision with earth, a collision which would result in the death of all of earth's inhabitants.

The story grabbed me from the first page and held my attention so that I was oblivious to the things I usually heard. I didn't hear the loud ticks of the large mantel clock, or the wind, or even the low rumbling far to the west. For thirty or forty minutes, I was completely engrossed in the book and then, suddenly, a chill that had nothing to do with the story shot up my spine. I could feel the shivers shoot to the top of my neck and travel into my scalp, and I had the sensation of my hair standing straight up. I was scared. Really scared. I felt paralyzed. I kept my eyes on the page in front of me and didn't raise my head. I could feel something staring at me, and there was no way I was going to look up and face whatever was standing outside the window. On the other side of the room from my chair was a brick fireplace. The hearth was at floor level. The chimney bricks rose to the top of the ten-foot ceiling. On either side of the fireplace were windows that looked out into the garden. Whoever was watching me was standing just beyond one of the windows. The book I was holding became a blur. A drop of sweat fell from my forehead and landed on the open page. My heart was beating so fast and loud I thought its pounding could be heard by anyone in the neighborhood.

I wasn't still very long. It must have been animal instinct that caused me to jump out of the chair, look toward the window, and get ready to defend myself. My eyes caught the windows. I couldn't see anything but blackness. When I think back it seems strange that even though I was still terrified, I didn't run away. Instead, I ran straight to the back door and out into the garden.

Nothing.

No one was there. Still scared but a little calmer, I slowly walked through the garden and beyond the house, looking from side to side. I saw nothing strange. The only sounds I heard were the rhythmic night sounds of the crickets and frogs, the wind in the old hackberry trees, and the rolls of thunder which were increasing in number and loudness. A spring storm was coming in. Only the ordinary seemed to be happening.

Even though I didn't find anyone, I was certain someone had been in the garden. When I went back into the house, I felt exposed, like I was in a lighted glass cube into which anyone . . . or anything . . . could peer . . . and probably was peering. I was sweating, my mouth was dry and I had a knot in my stomach. I decided to go to my room since I thought it would be the safest place. Walking up the stairs as quietly and slowly as I could, I kept my hand on the bannister and looked in front and behind. At the top, I stopped cautiously and swallowed. My bedroom door was shut. I couldn't remember whether I had closed it earlier in the evening. After a few seconds hesitation, I walked toward it. Slowly opening the door, I reached up to turn on the light and look inside. Everything seemed to be all right. Nothing was in the room that was not supposed to be there.

I walked to the closet door and opened it. It looked okay, but I couldn't see the back wall because of the hanging clothes and the suitcases on the floor beneath them. I sucked in a deep breath of air, then slowly pushed aside the clothes with both hands. I breathed out with relief when all I saw was the wall. I returned to the bedroom door, shut it, and turned off the light. With my back against the door, I slid down and sat on the floor. My eyes focused on the bedroom windows. I waited.

I strained to hear everything. The old house creaked everywhere, but I could hear no noise coming up the stairs. Through the closed windows of my room came the sounds of the crickets just as they had a few minutes earlier, only muffled by the glass this time. The frogs from the stock tank, a hundred or so yards behind the house, called to each other nonstop, and every so often I could hear the deep croak of the bullfrog giving his mating call. The thunder, growing louder, continued to warn me of the coming storm. The periodic barking of a dog at a neighboring farm and the thump-thumping of my heart were the only other noises. Through the windows, I could see only the outlines of the swaying tree tops and the flashing light from the storm in the west. I sat and stared at the windows for what seemed like hours.

The sound of the front door opening made me jump. My mother called, "Billy?" When you are thirteen, hearing your mother or dad's voice, knowing that they are present, is enough to exorcise any demon that is trying to get you. My parents were home. I was safe.

Over the years, although less frequently as I've grown older, I have dreamed that something horrible is chasing me. The dreams began when I lived in Dallas. In them I always run from a monster and attempt to get to the lighted room where my parents are sitting. I never get there. In my dream I can only run as far as the adjoining room. I try to call out to my parents, but I have no voice. I see them, but I'm paralyzed completely and can't move into the light. Only when my parents say my name is the spell broken. The thing that was chasing me then recedes into the darkness, and I am no longer threatened.

My experience that night was like a bad dream come true. My mother's voice saved me. When she walked through the front door and called my name, the terror, as in the dream, left me like air from a pin-pricked balloon.

"Billy, we're home," called my mother.

"I'm up here," I yelled from the second floor. Then I got up, straightened myself and went downstairs.

My dad took one look at me and said, "My God, you look sick. You're as white as a sheet. What's wrong?"

"Nothing. I've just been readin'. I kinda jumped when you opened the door. This book I've been readin' is pretty scary."

"Son, there's quite a thunderstorm getting ready to hit. I hope the windows are all shut," Dad said.

"They are. How was the open house?"

I returned to normal as I listened to Beth tell me what her schoolroom looked like. I listened to detailed descriptions of her displays, heard her recite her poem about winter, and looked at the map of Mexico she had brought home. Last, I looked at her prize, a collection of different kinds of tree bark, all labeled. As she spoke, I listened to her and watched her with genuine interest.

As you grow older with someone as I have with Beth, you can remember only with difficulty how they looked when they were young. The present and so many years in between interfere with our memory, so most of our images are formed from old photographs. My image of Beth back then is also formed from a likeness she had to a movie star. I still think of her as a little Judy Garland playing Dorothy in *The Wizard of Oz*. Except Beth was always one step ahead of Dorothy. Beth was already over the rainbow. When she lived in the city, she made sure that's where the dreams really came true. When she lived in the country, she saw it as the happy land where bluebirds fly. And her attitude served her well through high school, college, marriage and even in the years following the death of a young husband in Viet Nam.

My parent's return and my talk with Beth must have washed all of the earlier events from my mind, because when I later climbed the stairs to go to my room, I had absolutely no fear. I undressed to a boy's night gear, jockey shorts, and crawled into my bed, which was located in the corner on the opposite side of the room from the windows. The night chill in the house was enough to make the sheets feel cold and give me little shivers before I wriggled around and warmed up. I lay there awhile thinking about nothing in particular, watching the room light up and counting the seconds between the lightning and the thunder. Two seconds, two miles. One second, one mile. Then lightning and thunder simultaneously. The rain dripped, then began to pour off the eaves of the house. It splattered loudly on the concrete at the edge of the garden. The thunder became louder; the rain, harder. I loved storms. Fascinated by this one's power, I watched and listened as long as I could keep my eyes open, then I slept.

I have no idea how long I was asleep, and I don't remember what caused me to suddenly be so wide awake, but I do remember opening my eyes, propping my head on the pillow, and watching the storm. The wind was blowing like a giant whip, lashing the house in waves, smashing the rain against the window panes. I watched the drops spread out in sheets, meet, and slide down the glass. It was then I saw it.

In the window, diagonally across the room from me, was the silhouette of a person. It was not moving, and it was looking inside the house. Trying to be as inconspicuous as possible, I pulled the covers farther up under my neck, hoping it wouldn't see me. What I saw in the window looked like the negative of a photograph, except the figure was black and framed by the light of the lightning, which was flashing so quickly that it seemed never to go off. At first I was terrified all over again, then inexplicably the scaredness just seeped out of me, and I began to relax. A calmness swept over me, followed by curiosity. I looked closely. I guessed by the outline that I was looking at the figure of a female, but I could only see from the waist up.

After I stared for what seemed like forever, an odd feeling began to work its way into my mind. The silhouette became a "she," no longer a monster, and I thought that whatever it was meant me no harm. I know now why

I felt that way, but for a long time after that night, I couldn't explain my loss of fear and my almost-pleasant connection with whatever was out there.

The logical reaction of an eighth-grade boy upon witnessing such a phenomenon would have been to slowly lift his knees, unobtrusively push down the covers, get into a position where he can spring, then rocket out of the bed and run like hell through the door and down the stairs yelling all the way to his parents' bedroom. My reaction was different. I took off the covers and slid first my right leg then my left leg over the edge of the bed. When my feet touched the floor, I stood up and walked, one cautious step at a time, toward the window, never taking my eyes off the figure that it framed. When I was only four or five feet from her, she vanished. There was no movement to either side, just an instantaneous disappearance. I ran to the window and looked out. The lightning flashes illuminated the house, the trees, the garden benches, and the pouring rain. Whoever had looked into my window was gone. Naturally, when I returned to bed, I didn't go back to sleep for a long time. I lay there expecting to see the image again. It never appeared. I shut my eyes. When I opened them, I looked out at patches of blue and white. I heard birds singing. I had slept, and it was now morning. The storm had passed.

I suppose I should regress a while and tell you something about myself, my background, and the time in which I was young. My name is William Garrison Griffin, Jr., but I've always gone by "Billy." I was born in 1941 in Dallas, Texas, where my father, Bill Sr., became a history professor at Southern Methodist University after he had finished fighting the Germans in the North Atlantic. My mother, Ellen, as the custom was in those days, did not work outside the home. Our family had one car, one dog, one cat, and a small brick house on a tree-shaded street about two miles north of downtown Dallas. We also had a girl, my sister Beth, who was three years younger than I. Beth was conceived in between the battles of the North Atlantic, a little family mystery I had figured out long before I graduated from high school.

During the fall of 1954, when I was in the eighth grade, my dad made the decision to leave Southern Methodist and accept a job at a state college in a small town located about forty miles north of Dallas. Dad didn't take the new professorship for more money or for professional advancement. In fact, it gave him neither. He also didn't take it to please my mother. Mother was very content with where we were living. The grocery store, the dry cleaners, and almost all necessities of life were conveniently situated only four blocks away in a neighborhood shopping center. Mother liked her house, her church, her friends, and the cultural life that Dallas offered its residents. Neither was my dad's reason for moving an attempt to please my sister Beth or me. Beth

17

and I had friends, nearby parks, movie theaters, and a soda fountain in an air-conditioned drug store only three or four minutes away by foot.

My dad changed teaching jobs because he had, in his words, "always wanted to live in an old house in the country," and he could not find an affordable one near Dallas. My dad pictured himself as a modern-day Thoreau, and although he never would have gone "to the woods" to live quite as simply as his Walden hero, he adhered to the urban myth that the country washes away all problems, and "out there" one lives happily ever after. I can still picture him talking with friends, telling them about the purity and freshness and simplicity of rural life. And believing it. His quest never quite led him to such a blissful state, of course, because of dust, bad roads, mud, septic tanks, varmits, snakes and all the other amenities that coexist with humans in the wide open spaces. At the time of the move, however, those obstacles had never occurred to him.

I can be very precise about what happened to me during the particular time of my life I will be describing for the remainder of this account. When you have a fascinating and poignant experience, one which takes every bit of your energy, senses, and emotions, you remember not only the experience itself but also the minor details that accompany it. Ask any old, ex-athlete about a big game that he played years ago. He'll be able to convey to you a picture of every move made, the colors, the smell, the crowd, what he did and what he thought. But this short period of my life I can recall so well was, of course, not all of my early life. The years before I moved to Oakpoint, however, are just a jumble in my memory, a collage. The pictures are all there, but they are pasted on a poster board in my mind in no particular order. Even so, they cumulatively had a greater effect on me than my junior high years did.

The collage I have in my head is all Dallas. Its skyline, the most impressive in the South, with the Mercantile Bank and the Mobil Building with its flying red horse towering above the other structures. Shopping with my parents, all of us dressed up as everyone dressed up then in downtown Dallas. The canyons formed and shaded by skyscrapers, some over thirty stories high. The cafes. The movie theaters. The clothing stores with their soft, rich carpet and cool air conditioning. The noise. The crowds of people.

Long night rides home. Lying down in the back seat, listening to the muffled sounds of my parents' voices and the low, steady hum of the tires against the highway. Evenings on a blanket in the front yard with my dad, listening to the Dallas Eagles baseball games.

Wet from the water sprinkler, the never-ending water drops flying out in all directions, catching the sunlight, cooling a little piece of the earth.

Picnics. Aunt Jean, Aunt Jo, Aunt Emma . . . so many old ladies, just a few old men, all loving us and saying how big we are. The front yards of St. Augustine grass, green and cool until the drought arrived in full force.

Sitting on the hood of the car at a drive-in movie, spellbound as Judy Garland and an entire choir rose on a platform and disappeared singing into the clouds. Lassie. Trigger. Rin Tin Tin.

A group of black elementary school children singing "America the Beautiful," intently watching their director, their faces uplifted, the mouths articulately emphasizing "land that I love." My inability to understand how they could love it so much when so much was denied them. My questions to my mother and dad. Their answer that they know it's wrong, but it will change soon.

The four block walk to the red brick school, Stephen J. Hay. Shoves and fights with older boys. Taking the long way home to avoid the tough kids. Snow ice cream on the infrequent days when it snowed.

Waiting for a white Christmas. Settling for balmy, dry Christmases and football in the street. "Over the River and Through the Woods" at Thanksgiving programs. The boredom of church services. The unintelligible sermons where my mind drifted off to baseball, basketball, and football, my athletic stardom being interrupted by the invocational hymn. My friend leaning over the edge of the balcony, dropping a perfect, gooey wad of spit on top of the man seated in the pew just below us. My admiration of such daring and my loud laugh that broke the holiness of the sanctuary. The consequences.

July and August. Pallets on the floor. Ice cubes in front of the oscillating fan. Soaking sheets at night. Polio. No movies. No swimming. September. The never-changing smell of an elementary school. The first norther of the fall blowing in on an oppressively hot afternoon.

Driving up and down the streets of Highland Park where the rich people lived, oohing and ahhing at the Christmas lights and decorations.

The floor beside the comic book rack at the air-conditioned drug store. Sundaes. Cherry cokes. Vanilla Cokes. Root beer floats. Chocolate malts. Banana splits. Slowly turning the dial on the radio beside my bed. The St. Louis Cardinals. The Chicago White Sox. The Oklahoma Sooners.

Disaster . . . Waco, struck by a tornado that moved down the middle of its main street, killing more than a hundred people. The torrential rains far into the night and pleas for sandwiches to feed the hundreds of relief workers. A mine disaster in South Africa. Almost 300 men killed. "But none were white," said the man on the radio. More questions I couldn't answer.

And Doak Walker and Kyle Rote and Johnny Champion, S.M.U. football heroes. Red and white racing down the Cotton Bowl sidelines to another touchdown. The State Fair. Cows. Sheep. New cars. The rides. The dizziness. The Freaks. The pin-head woman and the nightmares that came later that night. The dust of the carnival. The color. Elbow-to-elbow people. The shouting of the barkers at the booths.

The blisters from the push mower fighting the tall, dry Bermuda grass. Lawns gone dry from water rationing. Black women in their white uniforms leaving the buses at every stop.

Always being chosen last in football and baseball. Striking out with the bases loaded. My Little League team losing. Riding the bench. Long practices. One inning of playing time. No girlfriend.

Sailor hats, marching, Naval uniforms everywhere. Where's my daddy? Christmas trees. Fried chicken. Potato salad. Pies. Birthday cakes. Presents. Hardy Boys. *The Yearling*. Walt Disney. Roy Rogers. Gene Autry. Technicolor. Newsreels. Cartoons. Atlases and encyclopedias. Pictures of city skylines. America on the move.

As I related earlier, I first saw the apparition in the window on a Thursday night. The following Saturday morning, when I woke up and lay half awake, I was barely conscious of soft talking that came from close by. I turned my head toward the voice and adjusted my eyes. The screenless windows were open. The curtains were flapping into the room, blown by a soft, north March breeze. Beth was sitting at my desk talking to herself.

"What are you doing in my room?" I asked in a not too pleasant way.

"It's nicer than mine today. The wind is coming in from that direction," she said pointing, "and in my room, I can't get any of it. Don't you like it? Look how it blows the curtains."

"What time is it?" I asked, not answering her question.

"About 9:30."

I can still picture Beth sitting on a short stool, fixing herself up. On my desk, in neat rows, she had brushes, combs, Mother's lipstick, and several kinds of makeup. Her hair was in a pony tail, and she was carefully applying an excessive amount of everything to her face. The smell of perfume was overwhelming.

"Let me know when my room airs out," I said as I put on my jeans and walked out the door.

That Saturday night when I went to bed, Beth's beauty items were still on my desk, neatly lined up, and I remember thinking how embarrassed I would be if some guy were to come into my room and see all that stuff. Before I went to sleep, the wind had either stopped or shifted to the south, so the curtains hung straight down, lifelessly. Because the night wasn't terribly cold, I didn't close the windows.

The next morning it wasn't the soft talking of Beth that woke me. It was her loud, mad voice accusing me of taking her brush and comb. "Beth, I did *not* take your comb and brush. Why would I want them?" I said, defending myself.

"I don't know, but they were right here last night. See the space? That's where they were. You're going to have to pay for them if I don't find them."

Even as I argued that I had not seen them, I was vaguely recalling their being there when I had gone to bed the night before. I never admitted this to Beth, though. And we never saw the brush and comb again.

On Sunday night, following the puzzling disappearance, the moon was almost full. As I lay on my bed, looking at the light it made, I realized it was going to be cold and I thought of the open windows. I got up to shut them. When I reached the window, I glanced out into the garden which was spotted with shadows and moonlight. I froze. On the far side of the garden near the corner of the house was unquestionably the silhouette of a girl. I was able to tell that she was looking up at me. I stood at the window, not taking my eyes off her. She was completely still for a minute or so. Then she vanished.

Whether imagined or real, I felt the girl's presence many times in the following weeks. Wherever I was, I sensed she was nearby. Sometimes a bush would move, and I knew that she, not the wind, had caused the movement. When an isolated breeze broke a still night, I would look for her. She made the creaking sounds that appeared after dark in the old house. Anything unusual I attributed to her. Even today, all these many years later, I still think of her when I hear what I now know to be only natural sounds.

I also saw her silhouette several times in the ensuing weeks. Once she was walking toward the hills north of the house. Another time she was kneeling in the garden on a dark, cloudy night. I was standing in the lightless kitchen watching her. From that angle I could tell she was looking up toward my bedroom window. I don't think she knew I was anywhere nearby. By the time of the fifth or sixth sighting, I began to formulate some conclusions about her. First, she appeared only at night. (As you will see, this observation was incorrect.) Second, she appeared to me as a silhouette if there was some light. Her clothes, her facial features, the color of her eyes were hidden from me. I decided from her size, though, that she was young, probably about my age. Third, she took things. After Beth's comb-and-brush incident, I suspected that this girl or whatever she was had something to do with the disappearance. I wasn't completely convinced I had seen a ghost because I didn't believe in them, but I certainly was impressed with what I had seen. And I knew I wasn't crazy. I had seen a ghost-like shape that definitely had the appearance of a young girl. I had seen the comb and the brush on the desk. Both were lying there at midnight. Both

---

were gone early the next morning. Also, the window had been open that night. From what I had read about ghosts, though, they could go through anything solid. So maybe she didn't need the open window as an invitation.

One day, trying to prove that my suspicions were correct, I slipped into my mother's room and took a half-used tube of lipstick from her vanity. Just before dark I set it on a lawn table in the center of the garden. The next morning it was gone.

After I discovered the lipstick had disappeared, I went to my room and took some change from my drawer. I rode my bike downtown, which was about five miles away. Like most Texas county seats, Oakpoint had a square with a large courthouse at its center and lots of stores on each side. Three theaters were on one side of the square. Another one, the Texan, was on the opposite side. One block off the square was the largest theater, The University. Each block had a drug store and on the south side was Duke & Ayers, a 5 and 10 cent store. For less than a dollar I bought a small fake pearl necklace. When I returned home, I hid it in my room until after dark. Then I took it out to the garden and laid it on a wrought iron end table. Just at dawn the next day, I slipped downstairs to the garden. The necklace was gone, but in its place was a bouquet of bluebonnets stuck in a Pepsi bottle.

You've probably realized by now that I have not said anything about telling my parents what I had seen. Not once over a year and a half period did I ever mention to them what was happening, and to this day I've never quite been able to figure out my reticence. For some reason it just never occurred to me to talk with them. It was as if I never had a choice. Something prevented me from even thinking about it. The restraint had nothing to do with my relationship with Mother and Dad. We talked a lot, and I probably conversed with them on a more personal level than my children do with me now.

I can think of only one possible explanation, and whether it's correct or not, I can only guess. Here it is: Once, in 1966, when I was teaching school in Montana, I knew of someone being inexplicably unable to do what he normally would have done. It happened this way. William Doig was a rancher who lived in an isolated area several miles north of the Yellowstone River near Blue Feather, Montana. He and his wife, Evelyn, had three daughters, one of whom, Karlyn, I taught in my seventh and eighth grade class. The Doigs invited me out to dinner a few times, and we always had interesting after-dinner conversations. A lighted dining room in a ranchhouse out on a white, wintry Montana prairie is conducive to good stories, and I loved talking about flying saucers, particularly in a place where millions of stars just seemed to come down from a jet-black sky and touch you. William listened to these stories and merely smiled a slight, skeptical smile. He knew cattle. He knew horses. He knew the land and the equipment he used on the land. William had spent countless nights beneath those stars, and if anything was out there, he would have seen it. He thought flying saucers were just fantasies held by silly city people.

One morning in March, before the school day began, I was down in the boiler room of the old schoolhouse talking with the school's three other teachers. Karlyn Doig knocked at the door at the top of the stairs and told me her mother wanted me to call her before school began. I called Evelyn, and this is what she told me:

"Last night William got out of bed and left the room. He didn't say anything. I lay there for a long time, and when he didn't come back, I got up and went to look for him. He was in the kitchen standing by the sink looking out the south window, you know, the one that looks out front. I asked him why he got up and he said he thought he had smelled some gas or something strange. Then he told me to come over there and look out the window. I did. There was a light out there. I asked him what it was, and he said he didn't know. He said at first he thought it was some poachers, but it couldn't be, 'cause the light was on a small hill, and the small hill is in the middle of a pasture that's a whole section. You've seen that section, Billy. There's no road going out there. Nobody could drive out there because of the deep coulees. Well, we watched the light for a long time. It just stayed there. When it started getting a little bit of faint light in the east, the light on the ground started changing colors. It went to a green, then to a red, then a yellow, even a blue. Then, as the sky started to light up more, the thing just rose up slowly into the air. We just stood there and watched it 'til it disappeared."

The next day Evelyn described the same thing happening again the following night. That Friday after school, I went out and talked with William, who told me the same story. I asked him why he didn't go out and see what it was. I knew that William wouldn't have been afraid of anything. He told me he never was scared, but that it had never entered his mind to walk outside. After the first sighting, he had decided to see it again the next night if it came back. But when the time came to do something the following night, something again stopped him from even considering an attempt to find out what was on his ranch. He also said that none of the animals, not even the dogs, made a sound while the light was there.

I think that supernatural or paranormal things must have some power over your mind that prevents you from doing whatever they want prevented for whatever reason they might have. I think that if I had told my parents what I was seeing, maybe it would have been impossible for the things that later occurred to take place.

ike most brothers and sisters, Beth and I argued with and bothered each other when we were young. We're very close now, but as sweet as she was when she was a little girl, she still had an uncanny ability to get on my nerves, and she was an expert at warting me incessantly. I suppose if she were writing her memoirs, she might say the same about me, but she's not, and my memory allows me to remember myself without some of the blemishes. I liked to read. Beth had an aversion to my being comfortable and quiet and engrossed in a book. When she found me curled up relishing a good story, she would ask me an inane question, and before I could answer, she would ask another, delighted that I had lost my train of thought. When she asked me to do something for her, the request always came at a time when I was doing something else, usually something enjoyable. Beth also liked to get me into trouble. Once she told on me for slipping out of the house at night. I had crawled out the front door (really on my hands and knees) to meet a friend. He and I had ridden into town on our bikes, long after midnight. When I returned home, in the darkest time of the night, just before dawn, my dad was sitting on the front porch hidden in its shadows. I saw him the moment I reached to open the door. There was no trial. There was no chance to beg for mercy. The punishment across my bare butt was swift and hard. Through my tears of both hurt and madness, I could see Beth peeking through the slightly cracked door. I retaliated a couple weeks later by dyeing her white, long-haired cat with several different cake colorings. She laughed as my punishment was once again swift and, in my opinion, brutal. But, in spite of all our normal sibling wars, it's not the annoying traits of a little sister that I remember most about Beth. I remember mostly Beth's worshipful face as she listened to me relate some story about school. I remember her excitement at seeing something for the first time. Or the second or third. She collected everything. Pressed flowers which would come alive when she told you about them. Buttons. Cats. Dogs. Birds. Pictures of movie stars which she would pore over hour after hour the way my sons now pore over baseball cards.

Beth was with me that Saturday afternoon in late May when I saw the girl who had been haunting me. I had decided to go to the creek and hike upstream a ways to see what was there. As I walked out the kitchen door, Beth came running after me and said, "Mother said that you're going to the creek, Billy."

"Yeah," I answered.

"She said I could go, too."

"You'll have to go through some big weeds and lots of dirt and maybe water," I said, trying to discourage her.

"That won't bother me."

"Okay," I responded, resigned to the fact that if I said, "no," Mother would overrule me.

The two of us left the house through the back door and walked northward across the gently rising fields. It was an almost perfect day. The north breezes and the south breezes were struggling only slightly against each other, with the south just strong enough to keep the air warm. Pure-white cumulus clouds, moving almost imperceptibly, made the blue background even bluer. The grass was still spring green, and wildflowers covered the fields. When most people think of Texas wildflowers, they think of bluebonnets. I also think of the yellow and black coreopsis and the Indian paintbrush and Queen Anne's lace. When I think of May, I think of days like the afternoon Beth and I walked. I remember the lush, deep green of the trees and vines that grew along the fence lines and in the creek bottoms. The early settlers who arrived in Texas in long ago late spring must have thought they had found heaven. But they were cruelly fooled. They didn't know that May in Texas gives no warning of August, with its unbearable heat and its dead brownness, just as June in the north gives no hint of the long, bleak winters ahead.

Walking with Beth was not a race. She stopped to look at everything. Not a bloom anywhere escaped her attention. I taught her how to make a whistle from a blade of Johnson grass, and I listened to its screeching sound the rest of the day. We stopped and made little caterpillars by placing the fuzzy tops of grass between the edges of our hands and slowly moved our hands back and forth, causing the little make-believe insects to crawl.

When we reached the part of the crest where we could see the creek, Beth sat down on the hillside, looked up at me, and said, "Do you ever think about what it would be like to sit up there on those clouds?" She kept talking, not allowing me to answer. "They look so soft and pillowy and comfortable. I wonder what our house would look like from up there or what you would look like walking around down here."

I responded, "You can't sit on clouds. They're like gas. You would fall right through them."

"But what if you really could, Billy?"

"But you can't," I said, resisting the day's magic that had already captured Beth.

I sat down and both of us lay back, our heads uphill, each of us pointing out different shapes that the clouds made.

Beth asked, "Where do you think heaven is, Billy?" She answered her own question. "Up there in the sky somewhere. But where? How high do you have to go? Above those clouds?"

"I don't know, but I've thought about it lots of times, 'specially since we've lived out here," I said. "Just now, looking up there, I've developed a new theory. Maybe when we die, we're just spirits and we're like gases and we're up there everywhere. Maybe those clouds are heaven, and the white is spirits of thousands of people who went to heaven."

"If that's true, what happens when there aren't any clouds?" Beth asked.

"There are always clouds somewhere. Maybe heaven floats over the ocean a while, then over Africa or South America. Maybe it moves around so all the people can see where they used to live."

I could almost see Beth's mind working. "That sure would make it less boring if you could see so many places. Like Australia and Switzerland and Argentina. And it would be nice to look down and check on your children and grandchildren. At least I guess it would. But how would you know which ones are yours?"

"I don't know, Beth, and I really don't know where heaven is. I was just imagining."

Beth decided to stay behind on the hillside while I explored the creek bottom. From where we were sitting, we had a good view of the creek. On the far side was a relatively flat valley a mile or so wide. Hills of the same size as the ones where we were sitting marked the north side of the valley.

The word "hill," like "mountain," is relative. These North Texas hills would be hardly a swell in the Ozarks of Arkansas or in eastern Tennessee or Kentucky. Even though I had a panoramic view of their tops, the tallest ones were barely higher than the tallest cottonwoods in the creek bottom.

To the west, before the creek wound out into the middle of the valley, the hillsides along it were heavily wooded with some areas where the woods were a quarter mile across. Little side creeks or gullies were densely covered by the trees and brush, and exploring them looked exciting. In most places, few trees grew north of the creek. What trees had once existed had probably been destroyed to make room for crop land.

I walked down the slope from Beth, and within a minute after leaving Beth, I reached the cut bank below which was the creek's channel. I climbed down the steep side, grabbing exposed roots to keep my balance, and at the water's edge, I squatted and looked. True to its name, Clear Creek was running clear, at least in the shallow areas where it ran fast. Each short stretch of little rapids, which were hardly more than oversized ripples, connected large, still pools. In those big pools were little fish. And probably snakes like the cottonmouth water moccasin, the awesome and dreaded snake that lives in the quiet, murky waters of every single Texas creek, or waits, almost invisible, stretched out on overhanging branches, looking for boys who might walk underneath. Not even the rattlesnake competes with the cottonmouth in creating terror in young boys.

A short way downstream, past a pool, I found a crossing. Four steps, from rock to rock, and I was on the other side. I climbed the outer bank and began to follow the creek upstream and westward, checking out each pool. About a quarter mile from where I started walking on the north bank, the channel turned north. The water coming into that bend was moving faster than at any other place I had seen. From the high bank a cattle trail made a cut in the dirt and led to the rapids below. In the stream bed were fossils of all kinds. I still have a few of those rocks that so intrigued me years ago.

From the rapids at the bend I stayed on the edge of the inner channel and worked my way back downstream until I came to a wide pool in which the water appeared not to move at all. On the other side was a small, white, sandy beach. Behind the sand were huge, bleached-out tree trunks and branches lying where some flood had deposited them years ago. Higher up were thin-leafed locust trees, a large, old water oak, and, of course, a cottonwood which was sending down its feathery droppings.

Taking off my shoes, I waded across and sat down on the warm sand. The water in front of me perfectly reflected the green foliage, the blue sky, and occasional clouds. I lay back and looked straight up to the tops of the trees directly above me. Then, propping myself on my elbows, I looked back at the water and the top of the bank on the other side. The water was as motionless as the sky. The sun was warm. The cicadas, or locusts as we called them, lulled me with their motor-like sounds of summer and I lay back again, closed my eyes, and dozed.

When I awoke a short time later it was gradual, my eyes opening a bit at a time, focusing on the sky then the water which was still mirroring the swaying trees and the white clouds . . . and something else. I blinked a couple of times to adjust my eyes. There, in the water, was a new reflection. I looked up quickly. A young girl was standing at the top of the opposite bank. My eyes met hers, and we stared at each other for what seemed like a long time. I remember that the girl appeared curious but also a bit startled or embarrassed at my catching her spying on me. She was about my age. She had long, sandy hair with a little red in it. She also had freckles, which the distance was unable to hide. Her dress was light blue and very plain. She was so pretty it took me awhile to get my senses back. Actually all of this occurred in a few seconds, but it seemed like a much longer time. When I was able to speak, I said, "Hi," and she responded with a little shy smile but said nothing. I then got up to walk over and talk with her, but just as I took a step she turned and ran from the top of the bank.

Following, I hurried up the bank, but when I reached the top, she was nowhere in sight. I ran in the direction I thought she was heading. After I got through the narrow woods, I reached a barbed wire fence which separated the trees from a large field. I climbed through the strands and raced out into the field looking everywhere for her. I thought she couldn't be that much faster than I. On the other side of the field, I ran along beside the trees searching for some trace of her. There was nothing so I gave up.

As I walked back toward the creek, I thought about the field. The field was plowed, and although some kind of grain was growing, there was still a lot of soil exposed. "Tracks!" I thought to myself. I went back to the spot where I had first seen her and started a meticulous search for her footprints. I walked back and forth in an ever-growing arc. At times I got down on my hands and knees like I had seen the Indian scouts do in the movies. There was absolutely no trace of her. What made this mysterious was the fact that I could easily find my own tracks. Dejected, I finally quit searching and started home, thinking of nothing but the girl whom I had seen and trying to figure out who she was and where she had gone.

From a distance I could see Beth standing on the hillside where I had left her. When I reached her, she asked, "What were you doing down there, Billy?" Not wanting her to know what I had seen, I didn't answer her question, but instead asked her what she meant.

Beth said, "I saw you running out across that field and running down that line of trees. Then you came back and walked back and forth and back and forth. You looked funny."

Since she had seen what I had done, I asked her, "Did you see where the girl went?"

"What girl?"

"The girl in the blue dress. The girl with the long reddish-blond hair."

"I didn't see any girl. You were just running by yourself."

"You mean you didn't see a thing? Not anyone besides me?"

Beth said, "I did see the old woman."

"What old woman?" I asked.

"The old woman that was standing by the trees watching you. She had on a big hat, and she watched you run across the field. She was an old Negro lady."

After I saw the girl at the creek, I had to know who she was. I had to meet her. There were some girls at school I "liked," but I never had the feeling for any of them like I had for this strange, beautiful girl with the reddish-blond hair. She was all I thought about. My appetite dropped down to nothing. I couldn't sleep. At night I would lie awake imagining being with her. With my radio turned low, I would listen to slow, romantic songs like "I'll Never Stop Loving You" and "Wake the Town and Tell the People," and I would dream of her. She and I would be dancing the Aggie dance like the high school kids did, the boy putting his arms around the girl's waist and the girl putting her arms around his neck, just kind of hugging all over the floor. Sometimes we would be going to the store downtown like I had seen some high school couples do. I imagined it would be heaven to pick her up and just ride around town running a few errands and maybe stopping and getting a Coke. I thought it would be an even higher level of heaven to kiss her at the front door or maybe even at the drive-in theater like the people did in the cars with the fogged up windows. But I didn't even have a name for her. As I drifted off to sleep with the night breezes flavoring my infatuation, names of girls would float by in front of my closed eyes. None of them would ever stop.

When my friend from school, Earnie Wayne Evans, came over, he and I would go out into the garden or out by the lone tree in the back pasture. Earnie played the guitar. We would get words to songs and sit around on weekends after his chores were done and sing for hours. Earnie was thinking of Nashville, but I was thinking of the girl. I knew deep down that she and the silhouette were the same. I would mention other girls so Earnie wouldn't think I was crazy, but my mind wasn't on them. When I had some money, I would buy presents for her. Once I bought a set of tiny ceramic dogs on a little chain, and I left it in the garden. It was gone the next morning. Another time I remember buying a little silver bracelet. I held it in my hand one night and waited and watched the garden from my upper window. She never appeared, so long after midnight had passed, I took it outside and hung it on a small branch of a crepe myrtle tree. Then I went back upstairs and watched. I fell asleep on the floor beneath the window. The next morning the bracelet had disappeared. Beneath the branch, on a chair, was honeysuckle still fresh and smelling sweet because it had been carefully arranged in wet grass.

One Sunday morning, Dad was sitting at the breakfast table drinking coffee and reading the Dallas newspaper. Mother was outside planting some flowers, and Beth was upstairs in her room. I sat down across from Dad and asked him, "Do you think that people who have died ever communicate with people who are still alive?"

"What do you mean?" he answered, his mind still in the editorials.

"Well, we always talk about heaven. Do you think people who go there are able to look down here, or come down here and talk to us, or give us messages or ask us things?"

Dad closed the paper and looked up. Philosophical questions always interested him. He smiled in a way that let me know he took my question seriously. "Son, you're getting into some pretty tough questions that people have been asking I suppose since the first man died," he said. "The conclusions have been as numerous as the stars, and I certainly don't know the answer. But I guess like lots of other people, I've given it some thought. The answer really relates to the question of whether there is an afterlife. If there isn't, then the answer to your question is unequivocally 'no,' because there wouldn't be anyone up there or out there to communicate with us mortals."

"But what if there *is* an afterlife?"

"That's what I was taught, and that's what I would like to believe and do believe most of the time. But it's difficult not to be skeptical about it because I've never had any experiences that would show me for sure that an afterlife or heaven or whatever you want to call it exists. I've never had a direct communication with anyone who has died. If I had, it would obviously be proof of a life hereafter." Dad paused awhile, then continued. "Maybe I should qualify what I just said. I'm not *sure* whether I've had communication with anyone who has died. I've had some feelings at times that I'm connected with something that's outside of myself, something that may be spirit-like. But I certainly couldn't say without a doubt that something beyond the grave has ever tried to get in touch with me." He paused again. "It could be, though, that in searching for heaven, we look for something we can hear or see like a voice or an angel or even a ghost appearing, and maybe that's the wrong approach."

"How else would anything appear?" I asked.

"That I don't know. It might appear through our minds or our emotions. I've always thought that maybe we miss out on spiritual connections because we don't listen or feel or slow down enough to get the message."

"What do you mean?"

"Well, let's see if I can give you an example. Okay, I remember one time hiking in Colorado. I was in my early twenties. I had taken a trail that was several miles long and very untraveled; in fact, I don't think I saw another person that day. About halfway through the trip, I was walking along a high ridge, and I stopped to rest and also to take a long look at the view. It was spectacular. And quiet. I could almost hear the quietness. After I had sat there awhile, I had a strange sensation that something else was there, something I couldn't define. I was able to see everything that should be there—cliffs, canyons, forests, lots of different kinds of animals—yet this something that I felt but couldn't comprehend just seemed to exist and to be either with me or watching me. Something beyond the tangible was there. At least I thought so. Maybe it can be easily explained psychologically or maybe I was having some sort of religious experience. I don't know." Dad continued. "You remember where I grew up in San Antonio, that old neighborhood off South Presa Street?"

"Yes."

"My grandfather lived there, too. He was a great walker and a great lover of history and places and nature. I couldn't begin to count the times that he and I walked the parks and streets or along the San Antonio River. There was one rich old street called King William, that's now kind of dilapidated. But then it was in its heyday. It dead-ended at the river. Granddad and I would walk up and down it, and he never got tired of telling me about the families who had lived in the big houses that lined King William. Granddad died in 1928 when I was sixteen, but I never stopped taking those walks. In fact, when I was down there last year, I took the same old routes. Many times I've had the feeling that Granddad was with me. It seemed much more than just a memory. I could actually feel his presence."

"But you never did actually see him or his shadow or anything?"

"No."

I loved to listen to my dad's stories and thoughts, but I had not received an answer to my question. Mother, who had come in and listened to Dad talk, told me that I should call our minister and ask him his opinion. I never did.

I met Earnie Wayne Evans the first day of school. He saved me from what could have been a disaster. That first day was one of the worst times of my life. A new kid in the eighth grade.

Loneliness is epitomized by a thirteen-year-old in a new school. The unsureness that I experienced because of my smallness and slowness in maturing was intensified by the new surroundings and the new schoolmates, most of whom took several weeks before even acknowledging that Billy Griffin, Jr. was a living, breathing person. The kids with whom I went to school were not bad or unfriendly people. At least most of them weren't. They, too, were going through that stage of life when everything changes quickly, seemingly all at once, and the main goal of one's existence is to be accepted, preferably by someone who is highly accepted by others—in other words, the popular ones.

My junior high experiences made me sensitive to those who are always left out. I can still remember the unreturned smiles during my first day at the new school. Still very vivid in my mind are the unsuccessful attempts at conversations, when right in the middle of my sentence, the recipient of my words would turn away and begin listening to or talking with a known friend.

Oakpoint had three junior high schools. One was the black school, Abraham Lincoln. Another was Central, and it was the largest of the three. The third was Texas Northern Junior High. It was a public school, but Texas Northern State College operated it jointly with the community. Even though its enrollment was based on

47

geographical boundaries, its number of students was limited by the college to three hundred. I attended the Texas Northern.

Like all small-town schools, my junior high had a cross section of the community, both economically and socially, and as in most small towns, a kid could and did mix with the children whose parents were in a different group from his own. The one distinct group in the school was the cowboy crowd, which consisted of many boys who lived in the country and their town friends who ran with them. They wore the obligatory boots, jeans, western shirts and hats. They formed the majority that rode the school buses, and they made my introduction to the school a miserable and frightening experience. Scott Harrell was one of them. I remember that he was short and muscled, and that he strutted like a little banty rooster. All I ever saw on his face was a scowl, usually directed at me, even before he had the opportunity to dislike me by knowing me. His sidekick was Don Jones, a shorter and thinner boy who must have spent his nights deciding how to be mean the next day. Don's only saving grace was his sister, Anita, who was the prettiest girl on the bus and one of the prettiest in the school, a gut cinch each year for FFA sweetheart. I would have looked at her more if I hadn't worried about being maimed by her brother for even pointing my head in her direction.

On the first morning of the second semester, Beth and I waited in the cold wind in front of the house for the yellow school bus. Both of us masked our anxious thoughts. We were looking forward to the ride and the chance to meet new friends, but we were still scared of the change. I wore my Dallas attire of long-sleeved flannel shirt, jeans with no belt, and tennis shoes with white socks. Down the road, approaching us like a slow yellow mole, came the school bus. As it stopped, as many faces as there were seats on the right side of the bus peered down at us, their details obscured by the fog on the windows. We climbed aboard but were unable to sit by each other, so Beth sat in front. I walked toward the back, self-conscious, not knowing whether to speak or just keep my mouth shut. I chose the latter as I found a seat near the back. Around me was stone-cold silence. I didn't move a fraction of an inch.

"Whadda ya think of the new guy, Don?" I heard someone say behind me.

"I don't know, but he don't look like he belongs around here," said a voice I assumed to be Don's.

I was so worried by then that I wasn't even sure they were talking about me, so I sat rigidly still looking straight ahead.

"Hey we're talking to you. The shrimp who just got on the bus. Are you deaf, too?"

I kept quiet for a few seconds, then I made a gross error. I turned around and said, "My name is William Garrison Griffin, Jr. What's yours?"

The place exploded, "Oh, Mr. William whatever it is, Jr. I can't wait 'til we get this slicker out by the goal posts. Those pants won't be on him too long."

It was then that Beth compounded my gross error. She came running to the back of the bus demanding that my tormentors leave me alone. After a stunned short

49

silence, the laughter and derision began again. It lasted all the way to school, and by the time I got off the bus, I was as scared and humiliated as I had ever been.

The morning flew by in a blur like the roadside when you're going eighty miles an hour. I couldn't think of anything except what was going to happen to me during the long lunch hour. From my third period classroom, I looked out the window and saw the football field with the goal posts rising ominously in each end zone like crosses waiting for a crucifixion. And I knew who would soon be hanging from one of them. I was aching for the safety of Dallas.

When lunch time arrived, I sat at the long cafeteria table not eating anything, hoping I could prolong my last supper until the one o'clock bell; but thirty minutes into the period, the lunchroom attendant let me know it was time to leave, and she shuttled me into the hall. It was there the hall monitor, a crabby old fellow, informed me of the rule that all students went out of the building if the weather was nice, and I could tell by looking through the glass door that there would be no rain or snow that day.

I walked outside among groups of my fellow students, all of whom knew each other and most of whom were laughing and talking, none of them the least bit worried about being humiliated and beaten. And none of them the least bit concerned about my fate.

Sitting on the steps, I awaited my demise, which came quickly. Troy McPherson, one of Scott Harrell's henchmen, spotted me first and alerted the rest of the cowboys. "Scott, we got one ready for the initiation."

The crowds of students gave the gang a wide berth as they marched toward me. I took off and ran like hell down the steps, across the cinder track, and toward the middle of the football field. They were right behind me, and the guy named Troy caught me first. He swung me around and yelled, "I'll hold him. Ya'll get his pants." Hearing that, I fought like a badger in its hole, slugging Troy two or three times before he had a chance to hit back.

Troy's gang then turned on him shouting things like, "I wouldn't let him do that if I were you," "Bust him, Troy," "Kick his ass, McPherson!" At least my swinging at one of them had turned the battle into a one-on-one affair instead of a ten-to-one massacre. It wasn't a knock-down, ear-biting, rolling-on-the-ground kind of fight. It was more of a sparring match than anything else, and since Troy didn't seem to go for my head, I just dodged around and tried to hit him from the waist to the shoulders. And I wasn't too successful on either offense or defense. He pounded me at will. My arms and chest and stomach were hurting terribly, and I was on the verge of quitting when I heard the outside bell ring. Everyone including Troy ran toward the building leaving me standing there like I was alone in Antarctica. And I guess I was, in a way.

The blur of the school morning became the amnesia of the school afternoon. I couldn't remember anything even a minute after it happened. Somehow though, at 3:30, I got to the bus and boarded it, not really caring what my fate would be. It couldn't get any worse. I walked back to an empty seat and avoided eye contact with anyone. I sat by the window, looked out at the college buildings, and tried real hard not to cry.

Someone sat down beside me and tapped me on the shoulder. When I looked around another boy said, "Hidy, I'm Earnie, Earnie Wayne Evans. You're in my English class. What's your name?" Those were absolutely the best words I had ever heard from anyone. Sitting next to me was a tall, skinny boy with a caved-in chest. His hair was jet black and slicked down with lots of hair oil. He wore boots, a cowboy shirt, and jeans like most of the others.

I told him, "My name's Billy Griffin."

"You live up there on Evers Road in the two-story house, doncha?" he said.

"Yeah," I answered. "We moved in the other day so I could go to school here the second semester."

Earnie asked me, "You like it here, doncha? It's a pretty good place, and the school's fun, doncha think?"

I lied, "It's all right."

wo encounters in late spring of 1955 left an indelible mark in my storehouse of memories. One involved Beth; the other, me. I'll tell Beth's story as well as I can, remembering what I saw, but mostly remembering what Beth told me.

Beth had a friend from school named Amy who visited us often. She was one of those little-sister friends that big brothers pay almost no attention to until years later, when the "little girl" has "grown up." Then the big brother wishes that he had given his undivided attention to her when he had the opportunity. But I was a teenager, and Amy was a flat-chested, scrawny, prepubescent fifth grader, so her appeal to me was nonexistent. Except that I liked her.

Amy had been to our house several times, and during those visits, she and Beth never strayed more than a hundred yards from the back door. I was always encouraging Beth to do interesting things (as if she needed it), so one afternoon when Amy was at our house, I suggested that they walk down to the creek since it was running clear. I thought they would have a good time wading in the pools. At first both of them were hesitant about going alone, so I told them I would walk with them at least as far as the crest of the hills above the creek. My offer assuaged their fears, and they agreed to go. We left the house, but once we were in sight of the creek, I turned back and went home despite their rather sad, little heart-tugging pleas that I stay with them. Beth later told me what happened after I "deserted" them.

She and Amy found a pool with a white sand bar beside it. Beth immediately took off her shoes and waded awhile before sitting on the warm sand and sticking her bare feet in the cool water. The small fish that lived in the creek bit and nibbled Beth's toes, then Amy's, too, after she was finally persuaded to put her feet in. The girls squealed and laughed as they tried to keep still and let the fish bites tickle them. By mid-afternoon, they were getting hungry and a little sun-burned, so they decided to walk back to the house. Instead of following the path that I had made, they took a shortcut through the tall weeds that for little girls were like a jungle. Beth led the way and tried to walk in a straight line until she met the path home.

Most people who live in Texas think that rattle-snakes inhabit dry, rocky country. Few realize that if a choice is available, the snakes will live near water. And in weeds. Beth never once considered that in the dense plot of grass, a rattlesnake might be waiting.

Amy saw it first. She said Beth had reached a small clearing, and that she happened to glance at Beth's feet. Lying there, coiled, its monstrous, triangular head not more than two or three inches from Beth's right foot, was unmistakably a rattler, the largest Amy had ever seen. Beth said that just when she was about to reenter the grass she heard an indescribable sound in back of her. She turned her head and saw Amy's horribly con-torted, blood-drained face staring at the ground beneath Beth. Then she heard the rattles. As Beth looked down, the snake struck her with lightning-like speed, then, almost as quickly, moved off into the grass in the same direction that the girls had been traveling. Although the entire sequence took only a split second, Beth still remembers it as a long, drawn-out, slow-motion picture. It was as if she looked at Amy's terrified face for several minutes, and when she looked down, the reptile hesitated for an eternity before striking. During all of this, Beth was like a helpless statue welded to the ground, unable to move in any direction.

After the snake had disappeared and the girls had seen the bloody fang marks on Beth's leg, they were at first immobilized with fear. Then, crying and screaming, they moved back instinctively toward the creek, where on the sand they both collapsed and lay sobbing until Amy regained enough composure to realize that help was needed. She pulled Beth up, and they slowly limped along my path toward the house.

When I had left the girls earlier, I had gone back to my room, grabbed a book, climbed one of the trees in the garden and perched myself in a precarious position on a large limb that I used for serious reading. There, I launched into the exciting finish of an Eric Ambler mystery. An hour or so later, I looked up when I heard a faraway siren crying out mournfully. The sound became louder and louder and soon had my undivided attention. I jumped down from the tree and ran to the front yard. Far down the road, to the east, came the wailing ambulance leaving a heavy trail of dust behind it. By the time it reached our house, Mother and Dad had joined me in the front yard. To our astonishment, it swerved into our driveway and came to a sudden halt. Two men leaped out and ran toward the back where they kept going toward the creek. The three of us chased them to where we found Amy and Beth.

Amy was sitting beside the path like a little rag doll cradling Beth, who was crying and vomiting. My parents reacted quickly. Dad held Beth. Mother comforted her. The ambulance men performed their first aid. Dad carried Beth back to the ambulance without stopping, while the other five of us followed like a caravan. Mother rode in the ambulance, and Dad, Amy, and I followed in our car. I vaguely remember the hospital emergency room and the pain I felt for Beth as the doctor cut her and drained the poison as well as he could. Beth grimaced and cried softly as they worked over her, but she was as stoic as any little girl could have possibly been.

Beth remained in the hospital for almost a week, and during that time she seemed to alternate between sleeping and throwing up, while we watched her ankle, then her calf, swell and turn an ugly brown. Then, as if coming out of a trance, her color became closer to normal, the swelling went down, and she was smiling again.

Now for the strange part. The night of the snake bite, Mother tried to find out who had called the ambulance. Neither Dad nor I knew. Beth had no idea. Mother asked the driver, and all he could tell her was that someone had called in. The next day, Dad and I went to the neighboring homes to try to solve the puzzle. No one knew anything about a phone call. Dad and I even went down to the creek where the girls had been, in hopes we could see a house that had a view of the site. We were unable to discover a hint about who had seen the accident and called the ambulance.

Another very bizarre incident occurred that spring shortly after Beth had been bitten by the snake. From town, there were two direct ways to get to our house. The road in front ran in a straight line east for about a mile, where it intersected with a state highway that came north-northeast out of Oakpoint. That was the route we usually took because it was much quicker, and there was more pavement. To the west the road ran straight for about a half mile. Just beyond the Isbell ranch, it curved north-northwestward and snaked along for awhile, following the contours above Clear Creek until it met an asphalt road that came straight north from town. Along the section that curved above the wide valley were several views of the drainages that flowed into the creek. Most of these low areas were heavily forested. At least, that's how I would have described them then, at a time before I had seen real forests.

North of the road between the Isbell ranch and the intersection with the road out of town was an easy spot to cross the creek unless the water was high, which was infrequent. At the crossing, two large, flat rocks blocked the stream. Separating them was a gap of about three feet through which the water flowed, a simple jump for a boy. Not more than a hundred yards on the other side of the crossing was an abandoned gravel mine which contained several acres of land covered with steep, miniature hills twenty or so feet high. Because the mining had ceased years before, bushes and trees grew out of these cone-shaped, rocky heaps, and it was a great place to hide out or to play any game our imaginations could create. It was also a halfway point between my place and Earnie's place and almost all other homes where boys lived. At night or late evening or on foggy days, "the mountains" as we called them, took on an other-worldly appearance, and many a time we sat in the strange atmosphere at the shaded foot of one of those mounds and discussed important happenings such as grisly murders, spacecraft, and ghosts of old Indians that roamed "the mountains." Sometimes we discussed the mysteries of that wonderful thing called sex, an event which, when participated in, would lead to a life of perfect satisfaction and happiness. On those days when we played chase or our version of hide and seek, I left for home high spirited, but on those occasions when the bull sessions were of horrors, I went home scared, taking the quickest route I could, trying to avoid running into all those unnatural and perilous things that might be roaming the countryside.

One such late afternoon, several of us had huddled between four peaks near the north side of "the mountains," telling "true stories." That evening, Earnie had brought with him a high school boy named Ronnie. According to Earnie, Ronnie knew more stories about the town and countryside than any other kid around. His dad was a cop, and his granddad had been one, too. Nothing illicit that happened in Oakpoint and was discovered by the police had failed to be taken in and stored by Ronnie for future telling. Earnie asked Ronnie to tell us some things he had heard and Ronnie obligingly began with the one about the girl who woke up one morning and found her headless roommate lying in the bed beside her. Then, while we sat there entranced, looking suspiciously around us, Ronnie related the one about the boy and girl who left their favorite parking spot because the radio was warning of an insane man with a hook on his arm who had escaped an area mental hospital and was considered to be highly dangerous. When the boy arrived at his girlfriend's house and went around to her door to let her out, he found the hook on the door handle. The crazed man was captured that night where the couple had parked, screaming in pain because the hook had been violently ripped from his arm when the boy sped off. We all sat there unmoving. For a minute that seemed like an hour, no one spoke. It would have been a good time to tell my own ghost story, but the thought never entered my mind.

After listening to Ronnie's stories, I left our rendez-vous that evening "scared shitless" as we termed it. My condition worsened just after I left their company and noises began to rise around me. Unfortunately, the sounds I heard on the way home were not concoctions of my imagination. Within seconds, catching a hint of something amiss, I stopped and listened carefully. A panting noise was coming from somewhere. I turned slowly, examining everything, but all I saw was pile after pile of old gravel heaps. The silence of the old pit heightened its mysteriousness and added to my fear that something was lurking there, waiting and watching and following me. The calmness I had felt when I saw the silhouette of the girl was missing this time. This observer was something more sinister. I resumed walking, stopping every few steps and listening. At one point I heard, off to my left, a sound I guessed to be gravel sliding, as if someone had stepped on it and pushed it down a slope. That was followed by a second sliding sound. The faint panting sound continued when I walked and ceased when I stopped. It was so feeble, though, that I couldn't decide whether what I was hearing was really a sound or only the silence playing tricks on me. I walked on, trying to act normal. Finally, just ahead of me, I saw the edge of the pit. When I reached it, I scrambled up the side then looked back just in time to see a split-second movement in the brush between two of the "mountains."

My eyes fixed on the eastern horizon, the direction of my home, and I commenced a long-striding, fast run that would have impressed any miler of that day. Like a trackman, I didn't look to the side or behind me, only ahead. But not too far down the road I caught something out of the side of my eye. I turned my head to the left and saw two huge dogs, one a German shepherd, the other, I thought, a Doberman, both running silently at my speed and looking straight ahead. I tried to pick up the pace, but as soon as I speeded up, the two dogs moved ahead at the same pace, all the while paying absolutely no attention to me. I ran faster. My chest began to tighten, and every breath burned in my lungs. My legs tightened and I began to struggle. I tried to relax by picturing myself gliding along. That was supposed to help me run faster. It didn't work. I was too tired, my adrenalin was running out, and home or even the Isbell's ranch was too far away. There was no way to escape, so

I just stopped right in the middle of the road and prepared to fight and die.

My stalkers stopped at exactly the same time, only a few feet away at the edge of the road. I was sure they saw the terror in my eyes. They walked toward me, tails down and still, mouths showing long teeth. Both dogs were making low snarling sounds. The Doberman rocked back on his back legs, stretched out his neck, and, ready to spring, let out the most diabolical growl imaginable. My terror changed to panic, but just as I reached over to grab a rock for a last ditch battle, a long, shrill whistle pierced the air. I looked up. The dogs looked up. They turned immediately, trotted off the road, crawled through a barbed wire fence and disappeared into the woods. I stood there a moment, trying to hold back tears, then hurried on home.

everal days after the incident with the dogs, Earnie, Gary Higgs and I were sitting on the sandstone boulders of the terrace just below the tennis courts. Gary, who would be my best friend throughout school, was in several of my classes. Even though he wasn't much larger than I, he was the best athlete in school and would have been one of the best students if he had been able to stay out of trouble with the teachers. I guess Gary's hair was really brown but he kept changing it. When I first met him it was black. Now it was peroxided. While Gary made markings in the sand with a stick, he said, "Think of it this way. It's better to be killing time than to be gettin' killed like you've been lately."

"It's just because they haven't found me yet," I responded as I threw little pebbles in an attempt to mess up Gary's sand figures.

"Nope, you're wrong," said Gary. "You have managed to demolish those bastards by losing every single fight, some of them even badly. That's the way it works, though. Once you stand up and fight, you've paid your dues, and they won't bother you again."

"He's right," Earnie chimed in. "They're still chicken shits, though."

Earnie was a good friend and was always ready to give moral support or consolation if that's what you needed. Gary could give you that and some legitimacy, too. No one messed with him. From what everyone said, he was the first kid to ride a bike. He was the first one to stay out all night. If the situation demanded that there be a fight, Gary always hit first (and last). By the time he was in the third grade, his pugnaciousness had deterred forever all attacks from anyone who knew him. He wasn't big. He just knew how to do everything. It came from living so many places with so many people and from running around with college boys. Gary knew them all and got his supply of sex pictures from them. And he was generous in sharing the pictures with his friends. I never got the story straight, but I think Gary's mother died or got real sick, and he went to live with an aunt. There were several aunts, and Gary moved from one to the other, changing last names whenever he changed addresses. It drove the teachers crazy.

Gary scooted over to me and put his hand on the right sleeve of his shirt, pulling it out like he was offering it to me. Which he was. "Smell this, Billy," he said proudly.

"Your arm pit?"

"No, stupid. The perfume."

I leaned over and took a whiff. Gary leaned back and smirked, "Mary Jane. Bought her some of that Shalimar perfume."

The meaning of Gary's statement was self-evident. Mary Jane Massey was the most desirable girl in school. Everyone had a crush on her at one time or another, but she liked Gary. I was envious, not because it was Mary Jane, but because Gary was so lucky to have perfume from a girl on his shirt.

My mind switched subjects, and, without thinking, I blurted out, "Do ya'll know anything about ghosts?"

"I know where all the right houses are," said Gary. "Even spent the night in a couple of them. Didn't see anything, though."

Earnie, becoming interested, said, "I know all the stories, but if you really want to learn about ghosts, go talk to Hebronetta Sikes."

"Who the hell is that?" said Gary.

"She's an old colored lady, and I mean old, who lives down on Clear Creek not too far from Billy. I know where she lives. It's in a little canyon-like place that runs off the main creek. It's real hard to see. You have to be going there to ever see it. I got close one time, but I got scared. She has some big dogs, and there are lots of stories 'bout her. Some people say she's crazy. My dad says she's smart as a whip, just uneducated." With less enthusiasm Earnie said, "He says I'm both dumb and uneducated."

My mind was racing like an Olympic sprinter. Dogs. The old Negro woman that Beth saw in the woods the day I saw the girl. I asked, "What kind of stories?"

"Lots of them. They say she knows voodoo and uses it sometimes. This old guy that works for my dad says that people who've gone down there have disappeared. Some people say that at night she takes her skin off, turns into a big black bird and flies all night up and down the creek looking for kids and things like that. She's s'posed to have all kinds of ways to talk with ghosts, and she knows all there is to know about them."

I had to talk with Hebronetta Sikes.

Saturday morning I wanted to be at the creek early, but too many chores kept me waiting until after lunch. Under the pretense of going fishing, I left out the back door. Out of sight of the house I dropped my line and pole beneath the big bois d'arc, or "horse apple" tree as they were commonly called. Using Earnie's sketchy directions, I crossed the creek and worked my way upstream, keeping to the adjoining fields so I could walk faster. Earnie had said he thought she lived in the third side gully up from where I would initially cross the creek. The first two tributaries came quickly, but I couldn't seem to reach the third one.

When it finally appeared to my left, I was almost to the point of turning back. Before I walked toward it, I looked for a long time. I was getting cold feet. I thought of big German shepherds and snakes, and Hansel and Gretel even crossed my mind. No one would ever know where I was until long after the oven had cooked me thoroughly.

Overcoming my hesitancy, I slowly blazed my way toward what I had convinced myself was death, or if not that, an imprisonment from which I would never be released. I couldn't find a path and had to pull myself along the steep little drainage that flowed into the big creek. That entailed grasping roots and placing my hands where I couldn't see them. There was no doubt in my mind that the entire route was occupied by big, fat, mad cottonmouths or coiled up rattlesnakes waiting for nothing else but to subject me to a horribly painful termination. The fear was short-lived, though, for no sooner had I rounded a little bend than I saw a way up the embankment. I climbed out and found myself at the tip of a very small meadow not more than ten or twelve yards wide. In the middle of the grassy area was a trail leading to where I hoped Hebronetta Sikes lived. I followed as it went through the meadow a short way then at a slight angle up onto a small table of land which was arrow-shaped, with the tip of the arrow pointing toward Clear Creek. At the far end of the little piece of ground was an old, unpainted shack which, because of the trees behind it and to each side of it, could barely be seen from where I was. There was no sign of life around the cabin. No smoke. No animals. No hanging clothes. No chickens. I called out, "Hello?" No answer. I took a few more steps, stopped a few seconds, then moved cautiously forward again.

Three short steps later, I heard a low, malicious growl off to my right. There, just inside the woods, not more than fifteen feet from me, were two ferocious-looking dogs, old acquaintances, the same ones who had run beside me in the borrow ditch.

Their eyes were focused directly on mine. Both of them seemed to march in perfect cadence right toward me, their tails not moving in any way that would suggest any intention but mutilation. Their growls seemed to ratify that message as they got closer and closer.

I heard myself whispering, "Oh God! Oh God! Oh my God! Help me!" He must have heard, because just before the chewing and slashing and murder began, I heard the same loud, shrill whistle I had heard up on the road. And just as then, the monsters stopped in their tracks. I looked toward the cabin. Standing in front of it was the strangest looking person I had ever seen. An old Negro lady.

"Whatchu want, boy?" she questioned me with an unwavering stare.

Gulping, I answered in an almost inaudible voice, "I was told you could answer some questions for me."

The old woman was silent. Without moving, she stood there for a while. She was short and rather stocky. Her face was enormous, with wide nostrils flaring out from the rounded tip of her pug nose. I couldn't see her hair because she wore a large hat that looked like one of my dad's, except the brim was floppy all the way around. She wore a short skirt, and on her feet were scuffed-up cowboy boots. When she told me to come on up, I did so and got a better look at her. Her eyes never wandered once from me. I had to look away from their piercing glare.

"Who tol' you to come up here?" she demanded.

"Earnie Wayne Evans did. He lives across the creek a mile or so away. He said you could help me."

Her cold piercing eyes were immediately transformed into grinning eyes, causing me to relax a little bit. "Well, come on up here and sit down then," she said, sticking out her hand. "My name's Hebronetta. Hebronetta Sikes."

I tried to be sociable, but both dogs had their muzzles at my butt, and it wasn't my idea of comfort. Hebronetta sensed my predicament and ran them off with some unintelligible word, then told me, "Don't worry 'bout dem dogs. Now dey knows I'm safe, dey wouldn't hurt a fly."

I stuck out my hand, and we shook. I hurriedly said, "Billy's my name, and I really need to ask you some questions, some things that Earnie said you'd know."

"Now what's dat boy sayin' 'bout me? What's it you'd like to know, son?" Hebronetta asked in a quiet voice.

"Do you know anything about ghosts?"

When I asked that question, Hebronetta Sikes looked at me, grinned broadly, then threw her head back and came out with a long, "WooooWeeee! Do Hebronetta Sikes know 'bout ghosts? Woo! Is de sky blue? Do de sun come up over dat hill over dere ever' day of God's long year? Do de possum put his shit in de woods? Do Hebronetta Sikes know 'bout ghosts? Billy, you come to the rightest place on earth to find out de honest truth 'bout ghosts an' thangs like dat. Whatchu wanna know?"

I was liking her already. "Have you ever actually seen a ghost?"

"Yes suh, I sure has," she answered proudly.

"What did it look like?" I asked.

Hebronetta, who was seated by then in an old, beat-up rocking chair, rested her huge head on her huge hands, leaned over, her elbows on her knees and said "You's jes' a youngster. I's seen lots. You's seen little. Before I talk, you tell me what bothered you to come up here."

Relaxing, I started from the beginning telling her about our move, about the night of the storm when I first saw the silhouette. She listened, hanging on every word as I told her about the missing things and the other times I had seen the ghost. I told her about seeing the beautiful girl looking down at me from the top of the creek bank. She heard everything I could possibly remember. She said she hadn't seen the ghost, but she had seen me running all around the field and just figured I was either crazy or just clowning. "How's your little sister doin'? She all right after dat snake got 'er?" Hebronetta asked me.

I finally figured it out. "You saw her get bit. You're the one who called the ambulance."

"Yes suh, I is."

I had suspected the ghost had something to do with the ambulance, so I was surprised and a little disappointed that this old lady instead of the girl had rescued my sister.

"How did you call the ambulance?"

"I has an ol' crank phone on de wall in de cabin. Dat connects me wid Missus Ingram's place. I jes' turns it roun', an' she answer. She old, and she home mos' de time."

"Hebronetta, please tell me about ghosts you've seen," I pleaded, by now suspecting that I had run into another dead end.

The old lady leaned back a bit then sat up straight and looked at me. "Well, da firs' time I seed one was when I's a little girl. We stayed over in Eas' Texas near Marshall. I stayed with my granma lots of times. She was an ol' lady who lived in an ol' house. In de back yard, she had a big ol' veg'table garden. Dat garden, it had everthang a person could ever want. Well, one

70

night, I wuz sittin' out on de back porch, and I seed dis black shadow out in de beans. It was all hunched over like it wuz checkin' out dem beans. I stared and stared and got scareder and scareder. Dat shadow, it jes' walk up and down dem rows lookin' at everthang. Well, when I got myself together, I run inside scared as de last monkey on de gangplank of a pirate ship, an' I asks my granma who dat was out in de garden. Granma, she jes' look up at me an jes' matter of factly said it wuz Granpa. I say, 'What he doing out dere? He daid.' 'I know dat,' she say. 'He jes' back checking on de veg'tables.' Well, when I heard dat, I run back out on de porch and sho' nuff, he still out dere looking at dem plants. I goes back in, and I say, 'Granma, how long he been doin' dat?' She say, 'Bout long as he been daid.' Den she tol' me why he came back. She say ghosts come back either to check on thangs or 'cause dey missed out on sumpin' while dey still 'live on dis earth. She say, 'Yo granpa, he miss out on his chiren growing up, so he jes' come back lots of times to see if dey doing okay. He sho' wanted to be a Daddy and his passing stop dat, so he jes' come back and do what he could. And when de chiren gone, he jes' keep comin' back 'cause he like his garden so much.'"

I couldn't believe what I was hearing. "Have you seen lots of others? What about right around here?"

"Oh, I seen lots. Sometimes I jes' feels 'em or dat dey here. Like dat sandhill crane flyin' low over de water up de creek flappin' his wings, silent as he can be. Well, he cain't fool me. I knows he a ghost. Don't know quite who he is, but he somebody other than jes' a big bird. Den deres ol' Mr. Thompson over der a couple miles away." She pointed toward the low hills on the east. "His boy come back at night, try to make amends. See, him and his pa, dey got in a big fight jes' fore de war, an' de boy he go way mad an' de pa he mad, too, and dey didn't make up. De boy, he got hisself killed over in dat big ocean by de Japs and he sunk to de bottom. His pa, he never got over it. A year so after de war, ol' man Thompson move off to Foat Wurth. Nobody live in de house after dat an' it got real bad shape. I's walking up dere one night, and I seed sumpin in de window. I goes over dere, and I looks in, an' sho nuff, it de boy. He standin' dere in his sailor suit jes' crying away in dat big, empty house. Crying for his pappy, I 'spose."

I sat there staring at Hebronetta Sikes. I was too spellbound by the stories to even blink. Her intensity convinced me that there was absolutely no doubt that she believed them. And I did, too, or at least wanted to believe real bad. Eventually I was able to manage only a weak, "Wow." She just sat there quietly looking out at the meadow. Finally I got myself back on track and asked, "Is there any way you can talk or send messages to a ghost and get answers back?"

"Now dat I'm gonna haff to study 'bout awhile."

"When can you tell me, Hebronetta?"

"Well," she said looking up at the sky. "See dat dry moon up dere in de day sky? It gonna be full nex' Tuesday night. Das a good time for me to tell 'bout de spirits. I tell you what you do. You wait out in yo' back yard and watch for de moon. Soons it come over de rim, you come, an' I mean right den, down to de creek. De moon it rise down here real quick after it rise up dere on de prairie. You follow yo' path. You know where dat big oak tree is not far on dis side de creek?"

"Yes Ma'am," I said, "The one with the big branches that reach down to the ground?"

"Das it. You jes' climb up de big limb on dis side and scoot yoself 'round so's you face dis direction. Then you cups yo' hans and you hoots three times like an owl, now das kinda like a loud dove calling."

"I can do that. Is this all right?" I cupped my hands and went "hoot hoot hoot."

"Das perfect. Now when dat hoot noise travel up here, de dogs de'll hear it an' de'll come down an' fetch you. Jes' follow dem back."

"Thanks, I'll see you Tuesday."

As I was walking off, Hebronetta called, "Billy."

I turned around, "Yes Ma'am?"

"Billy, you gots yo'self a ghost. A real live ghost."

eedless to say, the following four days contained the slowest moving hours I had ever spent in my life. It's odd that instead of occupying your time with numerous activities while waiting for something exciting that's going to happen, you have a tendency to do nothing but linger and follow the minutes as they gradually roll by. I suppose it's the same trait that makes us watch for water to boil or causes us to keep looking in the oven to see how the food is cooking.

Anyway, Tuesday was a long time coming. And when it finally arrived, the already slow-crawling hours came almost to a halt. So did I. My mother thought I was getting sick and tried to confine me to my room. At supper I only nibbled at my food, then excused myself, saying I was going out by the windmill to read. Luckily, in my family, reading could get you out of anything. And after we had lived in the country a couple of months, neither of my parents minded my roaming the creek after dark.

That Tuesday evening was unseasonably cool for June in Texas. It was almost like fall, one of those days that contained the last gasps of comfortable air before the real heat set in. I sat on the edge of the old, round, algae-stained water tank and faced east, legs dangling, my book in hand but my eyes fixed on the horizon. I was determined to follow Hebronetta's instructions as near perfectly as possible. I watched the sky as it began to lose its brightness. A couple of dim stars appeared, but the moon remained hidden beneath the skyline. What seemed like an eternity passed before the eastern sky began to glow against the darker blue of the early night. I dropped the pretense of reading and waited, readying myself to start my sprint to the tree. The sky above the rim continued to grow brighter, and when the first curve of the moon rose over the edge, I took off as fast as I could go, over the hill, down the path, and across to the big oak tree. I scooted up the large branch, turned myself around toward Hebronetta's house and went "hoot, hoot, hoot," just like she told me to. Then I waited. It couldn't have been more than two minutes before I heard a crashing in front of me, and within seconds the two dogs were directly below me looking up and wagging their tails.

Hebronetta was waiting in front of the shack when the three of us came racing up. She called out, "Tipps, Kern, here's yo' supper." She tossed them some meat, and they took off a ways from us to enjoy themselves.

Hebronetta didn't waste any time. "We needs to get set right now. You look over dere at dat gap," she said pointing. "In jes' a minute, de ol' moon goan rise perfectly through it, and I has to be thinkin' rightly at dat time."

I could see the sky in the V-shaped gap take on the lightness of a soft white as it prepared the way for the moon's entrance. "What do I need to do?" I asked.

"You jes' sit yoself down on dat chair beside de fire," she said showing me where she wanted me. "I'll sit on dis side. Now, don' chu be talkin' any, 'cause I cain't have nothin' blockin' de thoughts goin' out or de messages comin' in."

I took a seat in the weathered rocking chair, and for the second time that evening, faced east in anticipation of the moonrise. This time it didn't take long. And when it came, it rose with a size and power I had never seen before. The indentation in the hills produced an illusion that this was the largest moon to ever rise above the earth, bigger even than the prairie moon. It was as if I were witnessing a grand event that no human being had ever before seen. The craters were so vivid that they looked three-dimensional even from this distance tens of thousands of miles away. I looked at Hebronetta. Her face, like a statue, was fixed on the moon. Even the dogs were stone still, their faces transfixed as much as hers. The wood fire crackled. I rocked slowly and watched and waited. I forgot about time. I forgot about everything but the yellow moon. Hebronetta pulled me out of my trance. "I's got it, Billy. De message sho nuff 'rrived."

"What is it?"

"It's real simple like, but you listen real careful. You goan write notes to de ghost."

"What do you mean?"

"I means dis. You get you sum of dat school paper, you know, de kin' wid de light blue lines 'cross it. You tear de paper in four pieces. De firs' night, tomorrow, you writes a note. You say, 'Dear Ghos' . . . no you better not say dat 'cause I ain't sure a ghos' know he a ghos'. Jes' write de message. Ask anythang you wants to know. Den walk out behind yo' house to dat ol' horseapple tree dat stay out dere all by itself. Find de hole 'bout right above yo' head and put de note in it wid de writin' facin' up. Den take three steps backwards, turn 'roun three times and say dis:

'Possum in de creek
Cockroach in de jar
Tell me, ghos'
Jes' who you are.

Now don't you let nobody see you doing all dis or dey goan think dey gots one crazy white boy stayin' out here."

I repeated the rhyme several times while Hebronetta put some more wood on the fire. Soon it was crackling again. Hebronetta told me, "Now's time to come inside and get us sumpin' to eat."

"I ate before I came over here, but thanks anyway."

"Now don' you lie to me Billy. Dis ol' woman ol' nuff to know dat dere ain't no boy in God's whole world dat can eat a bite when he waitin' for a moon message. Now you jes' shet yo' mouth an' come on inside."

I did as I was told.

The cabin had a musty but not objectionable smell that was mostly covered by the smell of food cooking. It was pitch dark. No moonlight penetrated the cabin, so I stood near the door while Hebronetta lighted the lantern. The light glowed dimly then all of a sudden sprung out and lit the whole room. "My God," I said, "What in the world is this?"

"Dem's football pitchers."

"I know that," I said as I did a slow 360 degree turn and looked at the walls. They were covered solid with newspaper football pictures. Hundreds of them. There wasn't a bit of uncovered wall. I walked closer and studied them. I touched them and I could feel that there was more than one layer, probably several. "What made you do this?" I asked in amazement.

"I jes' always loved football. I saw a real live game one time when I's a girl, an' I remembers ever' speck of it right to dis day. I loves it so much dat ever' Sunday evenin' I goes up to Mr. and Missus Isbell's house and get dere sports pages. Den I comes back here and studies it. I cuts out de pitchers an' puts dem on de wall. My favorite ones I puts right here on de wall by my table where I can look at 'em all week."

"Don't you ever go to any games?"

"No, I don' have no ways to get dere, but 'fore too long I goan go down to Foat Wurth and watch me one. See dat radio over dere? Ever' fall I goes down 'roun' September an' gets some batteries. Then all through September, October an' November I listens to Mr. Kern Tipps on the radio. He gives de play-by-play on de Humble network, and I jes' closes my eyes and he takes me right dere. Jes' like I really dere in dat big stadium watchin' all dem boys score all dem touchdowns."

This was some kind of woman, I thought. "Who's your favorite team?"

"Well, I guess it otta be dem Baylor Bears since I be a Babtist, but my bes' team always been de purple and white of de fightin' Texas Christian University Horned Frogs. Dey plays in dat big tall stadium in Foat Wurth. It has seats all de way 'roun an' it sits right dere on de beautiful campus."

"I thought you said that you haven't seen a game."
"I ain't 'cept in my head. Mr. Kern Tipps, he jes'
describe everthang an' he puts de pitchers in my head."
I walked closer to the table. There, on the wall close
to a chair, were nothing but pictures of T.C.U. football.
"Nuff of football, boy. You come over here an' look
at what we're eatin'." On the black wood stove was a big
pot with steam coming out of it. I looked closer as
Hebronetta talked. "Dem's pinto beans, one of God's
greates' gifts to his people. You listen while I tells you
how to fix 'em jes' right. You gets 'em dried at de store,
den you soaks 'em, den you puts 'em over de fire an'
puts a little hunk of salt pork in de pot wid 'em. Nothin'
else. You lets 'em boil and simmer dere 'til dey jes'
gettin' soft, den you takes 'em offa de fire an' lets 'em
sit in de hot water for awhile while you making de rest
of de meal. Now de cornbread we havin' you do like dis.
You watchin'?"
"Yes Ma'am."
"You put de cornmeal in de bowl and get all de
weevils out. Dem de little tiny fellows dat run 'round in
de meal even if dey ain't got no air to breath. After you
removes all of dem dat you can find, you shakes de salt
over de meal den adds de boiling water jes' nuff wheres
you can mold de stuff into little patties. You see?"
"Yes Ma'am," I answered, concerned with what
looked like one of those tiny weevils trapped in the
patty.
"Nex', you put de patties in de grease, an' when it
gets brown on one side, you turn it over 'til it gets dark
on de udder side. Dese here are de mustard greens," she

said, pointing to another pot simmering slowly on the stove. "I grows dem in de garden out dere. When dey cooked, we goan put some vinegar over dem. Den we ready for de big dinner."

Within a few minutes, it was all cooked, and Hebronetta had me help her take it outside where we had been sitting, because she wanted to enjoy the coolness and the moon and the light of fire.

There wasn't much talking while we ate. Hebronetta was concentrating solely on the food. Only once did she speak and that was to say, "Now ain't dis real livin', Billy?"

I honestly agreed. And I watched her eat, oblivious to my staring at her. Her chocolate-brown face reflected the rise and fall of the flames in the fire between us. I had never seen anyone enjoy food like Hebronetta did that night. She would lift the spoonful of beans to her mouth, and when they entered and she started chewing, a faint, satisfied smile would break out on her like she was congratulating herself for every bean that she tasted. She would smile when she buttered the corn pone and just lean back and close her eyes in pure happiness when she took a bite.

Our meal finished, we sat there silently. The fire had died down to glowing coals. The moon climbed higher, and I caught long looks at it when it found gaps in the trees. The little grove of trees became a dark island in a soft yellow sea that the moonlight made in the meadow. Lightning bugs blinked on and off above the sea around us. I thought about the people who, for centuries before me, had gazed at this same moon floating in the heavens, and I felt a kinship with them. I also wondered about what might be floating around near us gliding through the trees and maybe even watching me. I wondered who this old woman was and what she was thinking about as she also watched the sky. I thought she might be figuring out who was checking on her this evening and who she would be coming back to check on before not too many years passed. I wondered about a lot of things that night, but most of all, I wondered about the girl and whether she loved me as much as I loved her.

"Oh, Lord!" I suddenly blurted out.

"Whachu usin' dat language for, boy?"

"What time is it?"

"Nighttime," said Hebronetta looking up at the sky.

"I know that, Hebronetta. I mean what time is it clock time?"

"Now dat I donno, 'cause I don' have no watch or clock. Why you wanna know in such a hurry?"

"Because I forgot to tell my parents where I was going. The last thing I told them was that I was going out to the windmill to read, and that was long before the moonrise."

"Lemme get the dogs and get you to de house quick. Kern, Tipps, come here right now and take dis boy back to de tree."

The dogs appeared out of the yellow meadow wagging their tails and shaking their heads. Soon we were off and running heading for the big old oak tree. When we got there, Kern and Tipps left me and took off one way while I ran like hell the other way.

Sometimes a kid gets caught, and sometimes he gets lucky, and gets away. It was the latter for me that night. I eased up close to the house and slipped around to where I could look in the living room window. Inside were Mother and Dad and two history professors and their wives. I could tell by my parents' demeanor they weren't worried about their son. I was able to get in the kitchen door, skip up the stairs and jump into bed in a few seconds. The last thing I heard that night as I was feigning sleep was the opening of my door, its shutting a second later and Mother's distant voice trailing off as she told Dad that I was in bed fast asleep.

The next afternoon, I placed my first note, writing side up, in the tree, stepped back three steps, turned around three times and said:

'Possum in the creek
Cockroach in the jar
Tell me, ghost
Just who you are.

The following morning, I arrived at the tree just as the sun peeked over the eastern horizon. The note was still there, but it was writing-side down. The next day, I placed the second note in the hole, and the same thing happened. The next two days, the result was the same, and I was beginning to get really down in the dumps. Failed expectations are difficult to handle.

Sunday afternoon was a blue day full of blahs, even though I had no work or school to go to the next day. After church, I just fiddled around with no interest in much of anything, killing time, wishing for the girl. Finally I overcame my inertia and reluctantly decided to go down and see if Hebronetta could tell me what had happened. I had certainly expected more than a turned-over letter.

Again I was heading for the creek. I climbed the limb and gave the hoot sound and was surprised when Kern and Tipps showed up real glad to see me. When we got to the cabin, Hebronetta listened carefully as I told her about the letters. She put her right hand over her mouth and cheek and mused for a minute on what I had told her.

Then she told me, "Billy, firs' of all you gonna haff to bring me de letters. I gots to study 'em an' see if I can figure out why you ain't got no communication. Now we gots a problem, 'cause dere ain't no moon 'til next month coming through the gap."

"Hebronetta, I can't wait that long."

"I 'spose you cain't. Well, if you come tonight, maybe we can catch a star rising through de gap. I ain't tried it, but maybe de star can give de answer as good as de moon an' maybe even if de answer be littler, it still be an answer all de same. Be down here right after dark."

I was on time. With no moon out, it was like a different place. Its enchantment was different. The lightning bugs had vanished. The meadow was no longer a pale yellow sea but a black void. The island was no longer the little stretch of woods. It had shrunk to only the small area that could be reached by the firelight. The darkness built a room around us. As before, we each sat on opposite sides of the fire, where we watched the gap for a star that just wouldn't appear. "Dey's coming up everwhere else. Don't know why dey won't come up in de right place," Hebronetta said.

I finally suggested we try another star even if it wasn't in the right place, and, after giving it some thought, Hebronetta agreed. She said that since she wasn't familiar with star wishing anyway, it might be that the rules were about the same. It wouldn't hurt giving it a try. Before long, we had picked out a rather bright one that rose not far to the south of the gap. Hebronetta went into something like a trance, and without blinking, stared at the star for what seemed like forever. Coming out of her trance, she said, "Han' me de notes in de order dat you put 'em in de hole." I handed her the first one, and she looked at it for a long time. "What it say?" She handed it back to me.

"It says, 'What is your name?'"

"Han' me de nex one."

I did, and she studied it for just as long as the first one. "What it say?"

I looked at it and told her, "Why do you come here? Are you coming to see me?"

"Han' me de nex one." This one she studied even longer. "What it say?"

"It say, I mean says, 'Are you the girl I saw by the creek? Why can't I see you more?'"

"Han' me de las one." This one she looked at quickly then handed it to me. "What it say?"

I hesitated a moment, then not looking up at Hebronetta I said, "It says, 'I love you.'"

Hebronetta's head rolled back as she said, "Oooh boy, we gots us more den a ghost problem now." She then swung forward, put her elbows on her thighs and her head in her hands. Within a minute she looked up at me and spoke, "I figgerd out the problem, and I gots de solution."

"What?"

"A ghost gots to answer yes or no. Dey don't have time to write out no answers."

"What does that mean?"

"It means dat you goan have to write a question dat de ghost can say 'yes' or 'no' to."

"How can I do that? I could spend a year asking whether her name is Betty, Lucy, Linda, JoAnn, Peggy and on and on. I can't do that."

"Yes, you can. You jes' gotta do some huntin' and find out who she is. I done some thinkin' on dis, an' it seems to me dat dis girl comin' back to yo' house 'cause she know sumpin' 'bout dat place. Now dat don' mean dat she not comin' to see you too. Maybe she be doin' both. I can figger why she go to de house, but I cain't figger why she come to look at you. But le's start findin' out who she is. I thinks you should go up and talk to Missus Isbell. She been here a long time, lots longer den me, an' maybe she can tell you 'bout who lived in dat house. Den you can ask de questions on de paper in de hole in de tree. An' by de way, put a pencil in dere wid de paper."

Hebronetta thought of everything.

Something occurred to me. "You know, Hebronetta, we've been talking about ghosts all this time. What if the girl is an angel instead of a ghost?"

"You jes' thinkin' she one of dem, 'cause you in luv wid her, but I's already thought of dat. You see, ghosts, dey kinda illusive. Dey invisible. Dey come and dey go, and sometime you sees dem and sometimes, dat is most of the time, you don't. And dey take on different 'pearances too. Now angels, dey don't do dat. Dey straightforward, like de one dat come to talk dat night wid de Virgin Mary. Dey be visible an' dey tells you what you gonna have to do. An' dey tells you what gonna happen to you if you don' do what dey tells you you gonna haff to do. No, dis ain't no angel, 'cause she ain't takin' care of you or guidin' yo' path in any way like dey do in de Bible. She wantin' sumpin' outta you."

I went to see Mrs. Isbell the next day. The Isbells' ranch was different from most of the other places around us. It had none of the junkiness that seemed so common. Even the trees were different. No poor-looking hackberries or horseapple trees surrounded the house. Stately poplars and huge cottonwoods, planted years before by Mrs. Isbell, distinguished their property from others. Inside the protective cottonwoods was a well-manicured yard watered by a well near its edge. At times when all other yards were dead dry or dirt only, the Isbells' yard was an oasis of green with flowers and weeping willows and even a rock-lined fish pond teeming with goldfish. When I entered that area, particularly in summer, it was like going from black and white to technicolor.

The house was an always-well-painted white, and its most prominent feature, the kitchen, was on the southeast corner. That corner had solid windows that looked out onto the lawn. I'll never forget my first visit there. It happened not long after we had moved. My parents had become friends with the Isbells, who were older than my parents by twenty years or so. Within a day or two after we had moved into our farm house, Mr. and Mrs. Isbell were there with a supper they had intentionally made large enough to feed both our families. I thought they were the most interesting people I had ever met, not only because of their stories but because they paid so much attention to Beth and me. Mr. Isbell was tall and lean and had solid white hair just as his wife did. He had been born on the ranch where they now lived, and he knew its history from the day it was first settled. His dad had told him stories of sitting on the hills behind his house and watching great herds of buffalo congregate within a mile of the ranch. In 1934 Mr. Isbell had killed an elk several miles upstream on Clear Creek. It was still the largest trophy elk ever taken in Texas.

If Mr. Isbell was a master storyteller of the old history, Mrs. Isbell was an expert in recent history. Not one miserable, old, broken down shack or big fine farmhouse had escaped her attention. She knew the lives of all who had successfully or unsuccessfully lived in this country. She knew what their hopes had been and where those hopes had led them. That first night the Isbells came over, it was well past midnight before their storytelling ended and Beth and I went reluctantly off to bed.

I had made my first visit to the Isbells' house on a cloudy, cold, windy February afternoon when Mother had sent me over there to borrow some eggs. In those days a kid could get a driver's license at fourteen, and since I was only a few months away from that momentous date, I was allowed to drive some in the vicinity of our house. When I arrived at the Isbells', the sky was so dark with the threat of snow that the entire house was lighted. The kitchen was bright, so I headed for that door. I wasn't more than a few steps onto the lawn when the most wonderful smell that I had ever smelled reached my nose. Something was baking in that kitchen. Mrs.

Isbell had me come in quickly, and after I sat down, it was an hour before I got up. She had a coconut pie and a chocolate pie on the counter, and in the ovens were pecan and apple pies. Waiting their turn were two of the most beautiful cherry pies I had ever seen. I sampled them all as she and I talked and watched the snow begin slowly and finely, then increase to large flakes, a rare and beautiful treat for Texans.

The visit that Hebronetta suggested, I made in July, the beginning of the time of year when Texans wish they were somewhere else. Mrs. Isbell met me on the lawn, and we sat down in the shade. I told her I was interested in learning something about the people who had lived in our house, and several people had told me that she knew more local history than anyone else. She agreed to help me as much as she could.

"Who were the people who sold our house to us?" I asked.

"Their name was Jameson. He worked in Dallas and commuted every day. I don't remember exactly what he did, but she worked over at the college in the President's office. Something to do with public relations. They only lived there for a couple years, and he was gone so much that we never really got to know them."

"Did they have any kids?"

"Yes, but we never met them. They were already grown and out of school and away from home when the Jamesons moved here."

"Who did they buy the house from?"

"The Lovetts. They were a real nice family. At least, we thought so. Had two boys and two girls. They all went to high school here then the girls went to the women's college and the boys went to Texas Northern. All of them graduated and are doing well. But the parents got a divorce and sold the house. We lost track of them after that. For a while, they both lived in town, but she finally moved somewhere closer to Dallas."

"What were their children like?"

"Oh, it's hard to tell. They seemed like nice kids, and they were all friendly, but when we knew them, they were in high school or close to it, and they were always on the run. I have some pictures of them if you would like to see them."

"Sure," I said.

What she showed me were several pictures, mostly of the parents, but a few of the boys and girls. I asked where they were now, and Mrs. Isbell told me they were in Oakpoint. She saw them every once in a while around town. She told me the Lovetts had moved into the house just after the war and had stayed there until they sold it to the Jamesons in 1952. The next family back had bought the house around 1938 or 1939, after it had stood there abandoned for six months or so. She had pictures of that family, also. Too many. Most of them were of little kids in all sorts of poses and conditions. They were swimming in little play pools. They were taking shower baths from the hose. They were blowing out candles. A grandmother couldn't have taken more pictures. All of that family was still around, and most of them visited the Isbells once or twice a year. Mrs. Isbell continued, "Before that, the Waldrops lived in the house. They were my favorites. The mother and I were very close friends. Hardly a day went by that I didn't see her. Mr. Waldrop was the last person to farm your place. I never saw anyone who worked so hard and tried so hard. And he always kept his spirits up when everything seemed to be going against him."

"What happened?" I asked.

"The tail end of the depression and a lot of dry weather. It just killed me to see them move. Their little girl was my favorite." Mrs. Isbell began to get a little wistful look in her eyes, and I could detect them becoming moist. She dabbed at them. "Their daughter would come up here several times a week and if there was a flower to be found growing anywhere around she would have it in a bouquet for me. If anyone in the neighborhood was sick, she'd be there ready to do anything to help out. When they moved from here, she was fourteen. I remember feeling sorry for her, because she didn't get asked to the big dances. I know a lot of kids didn't go, but she was so beautiful and the boys were really missing out. Didn't seem to make her any difference, though. She kept smiling."

"What was her name?"

"Catie. Catie Waldrop. She was named after her grandmother in Georgia whose name was Catherine. People always wanted to pronounce her name like 'cat,' but the 'a' was long. I have some pictures of her. Would you like to see them?"

"Yes, Ma'am."

Mrs. Isbell left the room, and when she returned, she handed me a large photograph with a thumbtack hole in the top. I looked at it without breathing. It was the girl.

And she was just as pretty in the picture as she was that day at the creek. I held the picture and stared. I looked up at Mrs. Isbell. Her face and eyes, which usually smiled, showed this time the signs of the sadness that always accompanies a long life no matter how blessed the life has been. A tear ran down her cheek. She must have really missed the girl.

The girl in the black and white photograph was standing, leaning against one of the trees in the Isbells' yard. Her long, light colored hair fell across her shoulders. In her left hand were wildflowers. She was smiling. She was beautiful. Trying to be as composed as possible, I asked, "How old was she when this picture was made?"

"Fourteen."

"Where is she now?"

"She died about a month after the picture was taken. In June of 1938."

I breathed in deeply, trying to contain myself. Mrs. Isbell handed me more snapshots. Catie with her parents. Then with the Isbells. In one she was picking peaches off a small tree. Another one was a first-day-of-school picture. Catie was always smiling.

"Here's the letter Catie's mother wrote me. I don't know why I keep it," said Mrs. Isbell, handing me a worn envelope with faded ink on it.

I opened it. It said:

Dear Kathleen,
I have some real bad news. Our little Catie died last month about a week after we got to California. She had

a headache that developed into a high fever. We got her to the hospital, and she seemed to get better. The doctor told us though that there wasn't much chance. She did stay lucid for a day or two, and we talked a lot about life and her hopes and dreams. Then one day she just went into a kind of a coma half asleep and half awake and then that afternoon everything just stopped working. She passed away early that evening, still trying to smile.

They say time heals all, but Bob and I are having a rough time. Sorry the news had to be like this. Pray for us. And for Catie.

> Much love to you and John,
> Eleanor

"You know, I never heard from them again, and John and I never found out what happened to them," said Mrs. Isbell as she dabbed at her eyes.

"Mrs. Isbell, would it be all right if I took a couple of these pictures and showed them to Beth?"

She didn't mind so I took several photos and walked home. I laid the pictures of Catie on my desk and looked at them for a long time. Then I hid them in my drawer in a book. I left my room and the house and walked out over the hills and down along the creek for hours, calling out "Catie" again and again.

PART TWO

Catie

Everything that happens in this
world happens at the time God chooses . . .
the time for kissing and the time for not kissing.
He sets the time for finding and the time for losing . . .

Ecclesiastes 3:1, 5-6

To see a World in a grain of sand,
And a Heaven in a wild flower,
Hold Infinity in the palm of your hand,
And Eternity in an hour.

"Auguries of Innocence" William Blake

"How many are you, then," said I,
"If they two are in Heaven?"
The little Maiden did reply,
"O Master! we are seven."

"But they are dead; those two are dead!
Their spirits are in heaven!"
'Twas throwing words away; for still
The little Maid would have her will,
And said, "Nay, we are seven!"

"We Are Seven" William Wordsworth

I got my first answer from Catie the next day. After wandering around calling her name, I went to my room and wrote on a sheet of ruled paper, "Is your name Catie Waldrop?" I placed the paper and a pencil in the tree hole and beat the sun there the next day so I could find the answer. On the back of the paper was a big "YES." That correspondence was followed by much more, until finally I wrote a note, "Meet me down at the creek tonight. I will go down to the big yellow rock and wait for you."

I was there after dark, and after sitting awhile and looking everywhere, I spied Catie's silhouette on the bank above me. In the weeks that followed, I sat for hours on the large limestone rock talking to her. And I use the preposition "to" instead of "with" because when I talked, Catie never answered. Still, I always paused for a few seconds, hoping she would say something.

"Catie? . . .

"I got your name from Mrs. Isbell. She told me about you. An' that you died. I'm sorry you died. I'm fourteen too. Are you still fourteen, Catie? . . .

"I'll be fifteen in June. Did you go to the ninth grade? I forgot to ask Mrs. Isbell. . . .

"My sister is eleven. She's in the sixth grade. Her name is Beth. . . . I guess you've seen her, though. . . .

"Can you talk, Catie? . . .

"I saw you down at the creek last spring. That's how I matched up the picture. How come I can't see you now? . . .

"I'll come down here all the time and talk to you. . . .

99

"Will you be here? I'll leave a note in the tree when I'm comin'. . . . "

The summer of 1955 was miserably hot and dry. But in North Texas that's expected. It's just a part of life. I worked four days a week as a soda jerk at a drug store near one of the colleges and I remember that almost every afternoon, particularly in August, the owner would make the comment, "It's hot enough to fry an egg on the sidewalk." And it was.

The heat and drought really showed its effects in the country. The leaves on the bois d'arc tree drooped like tongues hanging from a thirsty mouth. Along the creek the pools shrunk, and when the stream quit flowing, the water was separated by dust-covered rocks. The hackberries lost their leaves early, and the elm and cottonwood leaves turned an ugly yellow before falling off. The wind seldom blew, and even a small breeze was hard to find. The air just came down out of the cloudless, white-hot sky and sat on you.

Locusts chattered all day long, and water bugs skipped around over the stagnant brown water breaking the film on top when they landed. Flies swarmed around dead fish that had failed to escape pools before they dried up. Sometimes the awful smell of rotting watermelons and other decayed foods would find its way up the creek from the bridge where people had dropped garbage.

About the only activity Earnie and I had along Clear Creek was throwing large flat rocks in the pools. The rocks made the water snakes swim to what they thought was the safety of shore, where we chased them or shot at them with pellet guns.

Even though the beauty of the place was gone, I almost always made nightly visits to talk to Catie. If there is no moon, the country is very dark, and the dark is even darker along the creek. So I always took a flashlight. I was tempted to shine it toward Catie, but I never did. I didn't want to take the chance that it might cause her to leave.

September came and it stayed hot. I remember nights when I sat on the rock watching the shadow of Catie, her legs dangling over the side of the bank as she listened to me talk about school and other things.

"Do you like football? . . .

"I didn't go out for the team this year, but I like football. You know Gary, he's my friend I told you about. He went out and got kicked off the second day. One of the assistant coaches told him to go bring him a dummy. That's one of those things football players practice blocking on. Gary went over and got the head coach. Told him the other coach wanted him then walked back with the coach and said, 'Here he is,' to the coach who had asked for the dummy. The coaches didn't think it was very funny. . . .

"I *am* going out for basketball. I'm not very good, but Gary and Gerald say I can make it. Might not get to play a lot though. Dad is going to put me up a goal this weekend. At least, he says he is. I try to get Beth to play but she's too interested in music and science and stuff like that. . . . Do you like music? . . . Mrs. Isbell said you did. She even said your favorite songs were 'When I'm With You' and 'Red Sails in the Sunset.' My favorite songs right now are 'Mister Sandman' and 'Searching.' Tomorrow night if you want, I'll leave my window open and play them for you. . . .

"You know, our records we use are called 45s. They're smaller and have big holes in them. They're easier to handle than the 78s you used to have. See those stars up there? I've never seen so many stars so clearly. When I lived in Dallas I could barely see any. . . .

"Did you ever look at the stars, Catie? I mean, when you used to live here, did you ever walk out at night and just look up. . . . Mrs. Isbell says you did. She told me you knew all the constellations and you got an A on a report about them. . . .

"Catie, I was just wondering if you know more about the stars now than you knew then. Can you get up closer to them than you used to could? . . .

"Catie, I sure wish you could talk to me. . . . I feel kinda stupid sitting out here on this rock in the middle of the night. What if Earnie or Gary came walking along and saw me sittin' up here asking and telling all these things. Can you imagine how they'd look at each other and what they'd say about me? . . . "

My first days in the eighth grade were only an aberration. I made several new friends, and within a few weeks, I had ceased fearing for my life. Ninth grade went even smoother, particularly with Scott Harrell and the others gone to high school. But, because of a boy named Wanton Moore, things probably would have been okay even if Scott and his gang had not graduated from junior high.

Gary had been wrong when he attributed the cessation of my eighth grade fights to my fighting back. The credit should have gone to Wanton. He was one of those people who show up periodically in the public schools, then disappear after reaching the age of sixteen, never to be heard from again. During the last few years, several people have told me that Wanton still lives somewhere around Oakpoint, but only one has ever seen him. The others just "heard" he is around. The person who told me of an actual face-to-face encounter with Wanton is a policeman, who said that several years ago he answered a call and found Wanton near the side of an old, dilapidated building in the east part of town. He was lying there, his blood-splattered and beaten head cradled in his wife's arms. A tire tool was on the ground beside them. The policeman, as he was radioing for an ambulance, asked what had happened. Wanton's wife said he had been messing around, and she had taught him a lesson with the tire tool. Wanton had no intention of bringing charges, so the case was closed, and Wanton returned again to the anonymity reserved for the poorest of the poor.

In junior high we changed classes for each subject, but the same students remained together for each period. There were no honors courses. In those days teachers were responsible for giving extra work to the better students and helping the poorer students as well as they could. There wasn't much that could be done for Wanton, though, because his attendance was too sporadic. When he was in class, which was usually only the two or three days after the truant officer had caught him, he sat in a chair at the back of the room. He was too big for a junior high desk. He was 6'3". I never saw Wanton wear anything but a dirty white T-shirt and old, torn-up blue jeans. His tennis shoes were shredded, and he never wore socks. On cold days he wore what was obviously a letter jacket whose letter had been removed. Everyone knew how he had obtained the jacket, but no one dared accuse him to his face. Wanton had black hair which was cut in a burr and always looked like it was a month or so past due for a trim. He also smelled like his body and his clothes were past due for a washing; consequently no one wanted to sit by him. He had dark skin, the darkness of which was accented by a thin layer of dirt that never disappeared. Despite his size, however, Wanton never caused any trouble (except once), and he was generally good-natured.

I met Wanton a couple of weeks after I began school in Oakpoint. He gave me a stained-tooth grin and a nod of the head, and I responded with a smile and a "hi." In the following days we continued a daily recognition of each other. Once in English class the teacher called upon Wanton to read a short poem. As he started slowly and haltingly, the rest of the kids looked down at their desk tops and held their breaths, not wanting to show their embarrassment for him. I was sitting close enough to whisper the words he got stuck on, so he was able to finish the verses, at which time he broke into a big grin. Even Millie Standifer, the teacher, was impressed.

In those days, there were two ways that bullies attacked in the school halls. One method was "frogging." That's where someone doubles his fist then pops another just at the correct angle on the side of the bicep. If the aim is on the mark, the muscle will rise in a welt. And it hurts. The other method of attack was related to the style of the day. Boys in the fifties wore jeans, and they wore them as low down on their hips as they possibly could. The result was a style that I cringe to think about today, and one which made it easy for someone to jerk the jeans down. To protect myself when I walked from class to class, I always hugged the right lane near the lockers. My heart would go out to those unsuspecting students who failed to see an approaching attack and were left with their jeans around their knees. Sometimes the underwear went with the jeans.

About a month and a half after I had entered the eighth grade, I was working my way down the crowded hall toward third period math, when I saw three of my tormentors coming down the hall, shoulder to shoulder, toward me. Seeing their eyes fixed on me, I looked away and tried to melt into the lockers. As they passed, one of them shoved me hard against the wall. My books dropped all over the floor, and I heard lots of laughing. I tried to get up, and they pushed me down again. I reached for a book, and Scott stepped on my hand. I looked up, my eyes filled with tears, and screamed, "You turd!" Just at that moment, Scott went flying sideways. Wanton was there. Before Scott could recover, Wanton had landed a fist right in the middle of Scott's face, and the blood shot out of his nose. Wanton then grabbed him, picked him up and slammed him into a locker. Wanton stood there, an uncharacteristic meanness in his eyes, and said, "Anyone who messes with my friend Billy, messes with me. Tell that to all your chicken-shit friends, Harrell." Never again did I have a problem with that bunch of guys, and after a week or so they even became somewhat civil toward me on the bus.

I saw Hebronetta many times that fall of 1955. It was seldom a planned meeting. Usually she just showed up somewhere near the creek, or to use a better description, "just appeared." One time which I remember well, she almost scared me to death. It happened in October as I was walking home from Earnie's house. The day was gray. The stratus clouds looked like cake icing hanging upside down. The first frost of the fall had taken the green out of the earth, and winter was on the way. North of the creek crossing was a large cornfield I always passed through on my way home. On my previous trips, the corn had been either growing or it had been green, mature stalks. This time it was dead. I was walking beside a long stretch of the tall, dry stalks thinking about nothing in particular when a "pop" caught my attention. I stopped and looked around. Carefully, I searched the corn and listened. Another sound came. Something was moving. Something moaned. My scalp tingled. I took a few more steps. Whatever was in there seemed to keep up with me. A fluttering noise came from the patch, but no birds flew out. Again, groaning and creaking and popping and then whispering. A loud, slow whisper that I strained to understand. I couldn't quite grasp the words. By then, my whole body was tingling. It was getting dark, and I was at the wrong place at the wrong time. I turned to run, and I hadn't taken three steps when Hebronetta stepped around a bend in the path right in front of me. My heart felt like it had come to a screeching halt. I yelled at her, "You scared me to death!"

"Whatchu mean, me scare you?"

"You got in behind that corn and made those sounds and followed me."

She placed her hands on her hips, looked at me then shook her head in an "I don't believe this" way. Then she replied, "Billy, you is a city boy. You don't know nothin'. I gonna walk out here further in the path. You jes' step back about fifty steps an' keep yo' eyes on me."

"What are you talking about, Hebronetta?"

"Don't min' what I talkin' 'bout. Jes' do what I say. You gonna find out what make dat noise."

I obeyed and cautiously stepped backwards down the cornrow path, looking over my shoulder some, but keeping a wary eye on Hebronetta.

"Das far 'nuff, Billy," she yelled out to me. "Now start walking slowly, and keep yo' ears cleared and open, and listen to whas comin' out of dem dry stalks."

Quietly I came forward, listening carefully to the corn. Hebronetta stood still and silent. Within seconds, the strange cracks and whistles and whispering began again. Hebronetta hadn't been lying. She was silent and the corn wasn't.

When I reached her, she said, "Ain't you never heard of corn talkin'?"

"No, what is it in there? Ghosts?"

"Das what I's taught, but one time I crawled in and looked. Dere ain't nuttin' dere, 'cept de weight of de stalks an' sumtimes a lil' breeze."

"You mean you don't think spirits live in that patch? I thought you believed ghosts and goblins and spirits were everywhere. You got me talking to a shadow down on the creek like it was something normal, then you look at me like it's crazy to think something's in the corn."

Hebronetta again put her hands on her hips and shook her head in a disapproving way. "You in a real good mood, Billy boy. You jes' come on down to my place an' eat some of my cobbler. Dat'll get you on de right track wid de rest of de world."

We walked along toward the cabin, and I spilled out my heart to Hebronetta. She was the only one in the whole world I could talk to. "Hebronetta, I feel like an idiot. I've got such a bad crush on Catie. She's all I think about. I even went over to Central Junior High and stole a 1938 annual to look at with her. I write those notes all the time. Then I go down to the creek almost every night and sit there on the big rock, you know, that limestone rock down toward the bridge. And I talk to her. All I see is a shadow. She never answers. She never asks me anything. I'm running out of things to say to her. The whole thing is crazy. There's a girl at school who likes me, and I can't bring myself to liking her, 'cause I already have a girl I like so much that I just can't stand it. And my girlfriend's a ghost! I can't figure any way to get out of this mess."

Hebronetta was quiet, then she spoke. "I usually know de answers to thangs, but this one has me all tied up. I been tryin' to figger it out myself, but I cain't get no answer either. We know dat de girl used to live in yo' house. We know dat de girl come an' spied on you. We know dat she answer de notes you put in de tree. We know dat she meet you down at the creek. An' we know dat you seed her once on de creek bank. And fars we know, ain't nobody else seed her. You'd thank as good a friends she wuz with Missus Isbell, dat she'd seen her."

"Maybe she has."

"Whatchu mean?"

"Well, I haven't told anyone except you. Maybe Mrs. Isbell is like me and can't tell anyone."

"Huh," Hebronetta said placing her fingers on her cheek. "I never thought of dat. Nex' time I up dere to get de sports page, I gonna be quizzical to her, an' find out if de ghos' be comin' roun' her, too."

"I wish you'd quit calling Catie a ghost, and call her by her real name." Hebronetta gave me an understanding smile.

The two of us walked up the narrow cove to the cabin. All 5'6" and 120 pounds of me, and Hebronetta, husky and short, walking like a duck, her tennis shoes pointing outward. As we got in sight of the cabin, she stopped, turned, then walked over near the base of the small hill where she stood, looking down at a small wooden cross.

"I've seen that before. What's there, a dog?" I asked.

"No, dat's Homer Winslow Sikes, Sr., my husband."

"Oh, I'm sorry. What's he doing here?"

"He daid."

"I mean why is he buried here?"

Hebronetta sat down on a little rise beside the grave and rested her eyes on the mound for a few seconds. Her face had a slight, pleasant smile. She looked up at me. "It's a long story, Billy. Me and Homer used to live over in Eas' Texas. Thangs was tough, 'less you was in oil, and Homer, he like farm work. Well, he took off lookin' for work, an' he found it right here workin' for Mr. Isbell."

"How'd he happen here?" I asked.

"Kinda miracle like," she answered. "He'd looked for work east of here, but couldn't find none. When he come through Oakpoint, he stop by de market, you know, de one down east of de square."

"Yeah."

"Well, Homer he lookin' at the veg'tables."

"Looks like ever'one in your family looks at vegetables," I said kiddingly.

"Yes suh," Hebronetta replied chuckling. "It sho' do. But dat what got him de job. He lookin' at dem veg'tables an' tellin' de man thangs 'bout how to grow dem an' what makes 'em good an' all dat. Well, here come Mr. Isbell, and he start list'nin' and pretty soon

him and Homer talkin' and Homer, he didn't get no
farther den dis ranch."

"How did you get here?" I asked.

"'Bout a year later Homer he come back and got me
an' brought me here. Dat was 'bout 1941, just 'fore de
war. We move down here, den Homer, he pass in 1943
on June 2nd. Mr. Isbell, he asks if I wants to take him
back to Eas' Texas. Say he pay for it. I say no. Homer,
he loved dis creek bottom. I asks Mr. Isbell if he could
let Homer be buried down here. He say yeah, den he
buries Homer and gives me de deed to de little bit of
land, de cabin, an' dis little valley. So dat way I can stay
closer to Homer."

"Do you ever see Homer?"

"No, I never has, but 'member firs' time I seed you,
I tell you dat sumtime you don' *see* ghosts. I sure 'nough
feel Homer. I know he right here, an I 'magine he hear
me laugh and talk, an' he smell de food he like an' see
de trees an' flowers jes' like always. I goes out here
ever' day an' talks to him. Right now, I jes' feels him
all 'roun' here. Das why I wants him here, an' das why
I stays here, so he won't get lonesome or nuttin'." She
became silent in thought, and another small smile crept
onto her face. Then she slapped me playfully on the
shoulder and said, "Nuff of dis. Le's eat de cobbler, den
you get on up to de Isbell ranch and find out sumpin'."

Sometimes when I think back, remembering
Hebronetta smiling contentedly at me as I ate the cobbler, remembering the cabin, the steady glow of the

lantern, the creek, and my entire life back then, it's difficult for me to believe it really happened. Not only did I have an experience that, as far as I know, no one else has had, but I had a freedom in the fifties that kids don't have today.

In the summer of 1955 I got my driver's license. Like all my friends at age 14, I had the freedom an automobile brings. Back then we had the freedom to go where we wanted. Before I got out of junior high I had walked or biked or driven almost all the streets of Oakpoint. I went to dances, midnight shows, carnivals and softball games. I swam at the college pools during the summer and spent countless nights at the drive-in theaters. I roamed for miles along the creek and in the surrounding countryside during the days and well after dark. All of this was done without parents. And with their permission. My children don't know that life so they'll never miss it. But I miss it for them.

The day after I talked with Hebronetta I drove over to the Isbell's ranch. Mrs. Isbell was sitting on a porch swing reading a book. Ostensibly, I had gone there to borrow a book from Mr. Isbell, but my real purpose was to try to learn whether Mrs. Isbell had had any contact with Catie, and, if so, what she had told Hebronetta.

She looked up as I opened the car door. "Hi, Billy."

"Hi, Mrs. Isbell."

"What brings you over here today?"

"Uh, we're studying books about the Southwest in English, and Dad said Mr. Isbell has some J. Frank

Dobie books. I read *A Vaquero of the Brush Country*, and I wanted to see if he had another one."

Mrs. Isbell assured me he would have all I needed and lots of time to talk about them if I wanted to listen. As I started to go inside, Mr. Isbell came out, and the three of us sat on the porch. Mr. Isbell suggested a book for me, then discussed it at such great length that I was sure I could do a report without even opening or reading one page.

We talked about the book I had read and about ranching in general, then about North Texas history. Before I had a chance to bring the conversation to a point where I could become inquisitive about what, if anything, Mrs. Isbell had seen, Mr. Isbell abruptly changed the subject and asked me, "Have you been seeing Hebronetta much lately?"

I answered, "I guess so. I see her every once in a while when I'm down by the creek. Sometimes when I'm walking home from Earnie's."

"Does she seem all right?"

"What do you mean?" I asked.

Mrs. Isbell interrupted, "You know, Billy, Hebronetta is a real good person, and she's a lot of fun, and she likes you, but she has all these stories about ghosts. Claims to have seen lots of them. Kinda built up a reputation around here. Anyway, she was up here the other day, and she beat around the bush for a long time, then she talked about seeing strange things. I never could figure out for sure, but I think she hinted that she had seen Catie Waldrop. Whatever the case, she asked me if I had seen anything out of the ordinary lately. I said no, but she kept pressing. Finally, I told her, 'Hebronetta, I just don't believe in ghosts. If I ever saw Catie Waldrop around here, you would know about it, just like everyone else within a hundred miles.' I told her that that little girl is in the best spot there is in heaven and is not running around here."

"How does Hebronetta know about Catie Waldrop?" I asked.

Mr. Isbell told me, "We've sat on this porch many an evening and talked about Catie with Hebronetta. Kathleen will talk about Catie Waldrop with anyone at any time."

I looked up at Mrs. Isbell, and trying to be matter-of-fact asked her, "Would you tell me about Catie?"

She smiled and said, "Sure."

The three of us sat there that late October afternoon, as the day slowly slipped into evening. I listened, and I watched leaves drop then blow around the yard when an infrequent breeze pushed them along. I saw the sun set in a yellow sky, a sure sign of the beginning of Indian summer. Mrs. Isbell talked softly, the only other sound being the season-parting chirps of a few remaining crickets and an occasional interruption from Mr. Isbell, who sat in his rocking chair, his cowboy hat on, his glasses off, interjecting his own memories. I closed my eyes and watched Catie Waldrop as Mr. and Mrs. Isbell made her come alive again.

"Why donchu ask her out, Billy?" said Hebronetta as we sat at her table. The specks of dust swam between us in the shaft of sunlight that separated us.

"That's the silliest thing I ever heard of. Just where in the world am I supposed to take her? To Sunday School?"

"Hush talkin' like dat. You always bein' smart. You never think 'bout what she thinkin', Billy. Maybe she be wantin' to talk to you jes' much as you be wantin' her to say sumpin'. Whatever she don' do, she shore show up at yo' beck an' call. Dat lil' girl, she die when she only fourteen. She miss out on a whole lot dat you gonna get to do. Maybe she wanna take part in some of dat. It time dat Billy quit feelin' sorry for hisself an' start feeling a lil' bit sorry for dat sweet girl, Catie."

With some real remorse, I replied, "Yeah, I never thought of it that way. I guess you're right."

"I shore is."

"But whadda I do? I've never even had a date before."

"I donno, but you could start by askin' her to go get a hamburger an' a Coke an' some french fries an' whatever else ya'll eat. Jes' go down dere to de creek, an' when you sees her an' starts talkin', jes' asks her an' see what happens."

Hebronetta, as usual, was right. But before I could ask Catie to go out, I had to get the car. Although that was no problem, I did face having to answer some questions. I remember that evening very clearly. Mother

115

and Dad were sitting in the living room reading and Beth
was on the floor watching TV. (I was in the last age
group that didn't watch much TV. Beth was in the first
age group that became hooked early.)

"Dad, could I borrow the car for an hour or so
tomorrow night?"

"As long as you get your homework done first. Say,
do you have a hot date or something?"

"No, I just wanted to drive down to B&Cs and get
something to eat and see a few kids."

Beth butted in, "I bet you got a date with Susan
Morrison. Sally told me she likes you."

"Shut up, Beth," I snapped. "You and your friends
are always sticking your noses in other people's busi-
ness. I don't have a date with Susan or anybody."

"Sure," said Beth sarcastically.

Dad broke it up. "Just remember when you do have
a date, and I'm not talking about tomorrow, always open
the car door for the girl."

Mother told Beth to lay off when Beth told me to also
be sure to kiss the girl goodnight at the door. Before bed,
I walked down to the old tree and left a note for Catie,
asking her if she wanted to go into town the next night,
and telling her if she did want to, she needed to meet me
in front of the house at eight o'clock. Then I went back
home feeling stupid.

The next evening Catie revealed herself in a new and
different way. I'll try to describe it as well as I can.
When I remember that night, I still think that no first

date with anyone could have been as anxiety-producing as my date with Catie. No father at the front door, standing there to greet me, could have made me more nervous. I was scared. Scared of what might happen. If a shadow showed up, I was afraid my parents would see. I wondered how I could drive in and park and order curb service, then have some of my friends walk by and see, sitting in the front seat, a black shadow. I would become the most talked-about kid in school, and I could never explain what had happened without being committed to the asylum. In addition to all of my own fears, I really didn't want to hurt Catie's feelings, either. So, with all of those jumbled-up emotions, I waited.

Trying to time everything just right, I watched the clock intently. At two minutes before eight, I walked out the front door with nothing more than a quiet "see you in an hour or so." No one responded. No one paid any attention to me.

The car was parked between the corner of the house and the road. Upon reaching the driveway, I automatically went to the driver's side, then remembering what Dad had said, I self-consciously walked to the other side and opened the door. I stood there for a few seconds, feeling like every person in the entire world was watching me and wondering what I was doing, standing there holding the passenger door open. It was at that moment that I felt something almost indescribable. Previously, I had seen a silhouette which, in the garden and down along the creek, had developed dimensions and become a shadow. Once I had actually seen Catie on the creek bank. I had also received cryptic one-word answers to

117

the questions I had written on the notebook paper. This time was different. As I stood there, an unbelievably strong feeling of another's presence overwhelmed me. The first thing I noticed was that the backs of my hands and my face felt like tiny drops of water were hitting them. I had felt that before but until that night I had never associated it with Catie. I then caught a faint whiff of perfume, and after that I had flashing visions of Catie, so fleeting that they were almost subliminal. But I did see her. I knew that she had walked to the car door, gotten in and sat down. I was in shock. She was really there.

As I turned around to walk to the driver's side, something caught my eye, and I looked up. Beth was at her upstairs-window staring down at me, a puzzled look on her face.

I backed out, went down the gravel road to the highway, and drove silently down the long stretch of road that led to town. Ahead, in the distance, lights twinkled across the southern horizon. The November moon, egg-shaped and two or three days past its fullness, rested in the eastern sky making the man in the moon look like a fallen Humpty-Dumpty.

I groped for something to say. "Catie, see that moon? Looks like an egg, doesn't it? . . .

"The Isbells said that when you were a little girl, you knew all the Mother Goose nursery rhymes, 'specially those about the moon. They said they couldn't tell when you started reading 'cause you knew the verses and could look at the pictures and say everything perfectly."

We drove on, the only sounds being those of the engine and the tires on the highway.

"You went to Davy Crockett Elementary, didn't you? We'll drive by there so you can see it. . . ."

Crockett School was an ugly, non-descript building that stood at one side of the school yard. It was made of stone that looked like cinder blocks. Not a blade of grass grew on its grounds, all of it having been trampled by years of small feet. I stopped the car, and after stepping out, I went to the other side and opened the door for Catie. We walked in the dark around the old building. Since I hadn't gone to school there, no intense feelings welled up inside me, but even at fourteen, I was beginning to have an affection for old structures that would later lead to a deep sense of communion with their earlier occupants. I suppose my dad's love of history was being passed down to me.

I talked very little. I didn't want to disturb Catie's recollections, whatever they might be. They must have been vivid, though, since after Crockett she had only three more years of memories to fill her mind.

On the far side of the school, I sat down. I felt Catie beside me. In front and above us were windows decorated for Thanksgiving. I asked her about her teachers and friends and wondered aloud where they might all be now. I told her I would ask Mrs. Isbell the names and whereabouts of some of her classmates, then she and I could drive around town and see where they now lived. Mrs. Isbell said Catie always had lots of friends, who had come with her to the Isbells' ranch for visits.

Looking up at the three-story school looming above me, I imagined the images that must have been parading through Catie's mind . . . plays, singing, laughter with friends, tears, recesses, giggling, hurts, fears, happiness and all the other events and emotions that fill six years of elementary school.

When we left Crockett, we drove to Central Junior High, a red brick structure set in the middle of a campus, just south of the high school. I explained to Catie, "The junior high I go to is on the other side of town. Sometime we'll go over there." I continued, "My basketball coach says Central is really going to be good this year. He says they'll beat us 'cause we're too slow and short. He's probably right, 'specially if I play." I added, "The other day, I lost the ball three straight times. Coach says I play like I have gloves on. Gary can really play. He ought to. He practices all the time." I asked Catie, "Did Central have a good team when you were there? . . .

"Mrs. Isbell said you wouldn't try out for cheerleader 'cause you were too shy. She said you'd really be good. I know how you feel, though. If Gary and Riley hadn't almost forced me, I would have never gone out for basketball. Difference is, you would've been good, and I don't think I'll ever be much. . . .

"Mother tells me not to worry though. She says it's not everything and I've got other things I can do just as good. Did your parents use to tell you stuff like that? . . .

"I guess I'll do the same thing with my kids, won't you?" I caught myself. "I'm sorry Catie. I didn't mean to say that. I guess it's just that it's like you're really here." I caught myself again. "I can't say anything right, can I? . . .

"Mrs. Isbell said you were really funny. Always joking. Always kidding. I hope you can see something funny about my talking to you. Just think if someone walked by this car and heard me. Wouldn't be long before I got quite a reputation in this town, would it? . . ."

If Gary ever had any inclination to think I was weird, it would have been because of what he saw and heard the night of my first date with Catie.

Burgers and Cream Drive-In (we called it B&C) was located north of the downtown square, in the center of a block, bounded on the west by the street that went north to Oklahoma and on the east by the one that led to the Sidney Highway. B&C occupied only a small, narrow space in a large, one-story building that covered most of the block. Inside, several booths lined one wall, and the fountain and grill stretched along the other side. Two pinball machines, which could be seen through the plate glass windows, were at the front, opposite the cash register. The juke box was at the back. Most of the time we stayed outside and got curb service. I don't remember the place ever having a female car hop. The owners always used boys and men who were usually relatives. And the owners allowed kids to charge. It is inconceivable that, today, a drive-in short-order cafe would put a meal on the tab for a teenager. But that's the way it was back then.

B&C was a gathering place, not only for those who bought something to eat or drink, but for those who met others to get together and go riding around. The entire block surrounding the drive-in was usually full with parked cars, the drivers of which were somewhere else in town with their friends. Most of the kids who patronized B&C were high school students, but each year a new group of junior high ninth graders would begin to hang out there.

I found a vacant spot, turned left and pulled up to the curb, a few cars down from the entrance. I did a quick survey and saw only older students, no one I knew. I honked and turned on my headlights to signal a car hop. When Warren, the uncle of the owner, came to the car, I nonchalantly ordered two cherry cokes and a double order of fries, to which Warren replied, "Eating heavy, aren't you, Billy? Ha. Ha. Ha." Warren and all the other employees knew everyone's name. It made me feel proud to drive in and be recognized. Particularly with Catie there.

The fries and Cokes arrived. I told Warren to charge it, and he said 'sure' and wrote down the amount. I had some cash, but I figured Catie would be impressed knowing I was able to charge the food to my account. Being unsure what to do with the food when Warren brought it out, I placed one order of fries between me and Catie and balanced her Coke on the floor in front of the seat. As I ate, I told her about the place and about some of my friends. I kept eyeing her Coke and fries hoping they would magically disappear, but they just sat there, untouched. I told Catie that even if she couldn't eat them, maybe she could smell them. I told her that I bet the smell of fries would bring back good memories.

Next time, when I had more money, I said, I would buy
a hamburger. I knew its aroma would make earth even
more heavenly than heaven.

I was lost in talking to Catie, when someone jerked
and pounded on the locked passenger-side door, trying
to get in. I looked over and saw Gary beating on the
window. During my one-sided conversation, I had forgotten about everything else, and Gary just about scared
me to death. I told him to get in the back. He slid in.
"Whatchu been doing, Billy boy? Looked like you were
talking to yourself in here. Things aren't that lonesome
out there on the ranch, are they?"

"No, they're not." I caught myself. "The front door's
broken. That's why I couldn't let you in."

"I can't believe you're in town," said Gary. "Why
didn't you call an' come by?"

I answered, "I didn't have time tonight. Next time I
will." The conversation was making me nervous.

We became quiet for a few moments, then Gary
ruined the night for me. "Have you driven by the
Morrison's house? I'll bet Susan would go with you in
a second's notice." Now I was in a real predicament. If
I said too much, it would seem like I was covering up
a romance with Susan. If I said too little, Gary would
take my silence as an admission that I did like her. I did
all I could. I stumbled around and joked.

"You're real funny, Gary. Always trying to kid
about that Susan whats-her-name. You must like her."

It got worse. "You've got the shortest memory. It
wasn't a week ago you were asking about her. Speaking
of girls. Here comes Margaret. Look at those boo . . ."

I almost tore the horn off, honking, and almost ripped the tray off the window when I tried to roll it up. I hit Catie's drink, spilling it all over the front floor board.

"My God, Gary, I gotta go. I'm late!"

"For what? It's only 9:15."

"I know. I told Dad I'd be back now."

Gary opened the door and jumped out. "See you later, if you're alive. Slow down and remember while you're driving home your ol' buddy will be talking to Margaret and looking at those. . . ."

I burned out in reverse, taking the tray with me and forgetting all about it until I was several blocks away. I was almost out of town before I regained enough composure to talk with Catie.

"I'm sorry," I said. "If I had known Gary was going to talk like that, I wouldn't have let him in the car." Although I was embarrassed because of his comments about Margaret, his references to Susan were bothering me even more. I was mixed up.

Those little incidents that become so humorous and insignificant when you think of them years later, are so agonizing when you are experiencing them for the first time.

We drove the rest of the way home in silence. Not knowing Catie's thoughts made things even worse. When I parked at the house, I walked toward the old tree where I told her good night, then I returned to my room sad and depressed. I had done everything wrong.

I was not down for long. Sitting in the garden on a warm, late November day, I sensed Catie's presence. My spirits again went into orbit, and within a couple of days I had asked her to go out again. The second date was a library date. I had to go to the city library one night to find some books for a report, so I left a note in the tree, asking Catie to go with me. At the car, I had the same sensations of the pin-like pricks of water and the smell of perfume. I've often wondered whether what I thought was water instead was some sort of electrical charge.

The library was almost empty, particularly in the stacks. I had gone there to find some articles and books on caverns, but I had been sidetracked in the bound volumes of *National Geographic*. I even forgot Catie for awhile. My mind was somewhere in the outback of Australia when a loud crash startled me, and I jumped back to the present and Texas. Four or five books on the shelf behind me had fallen to the floor. I picked them up and put them back on the shelf in proper order. Taking out another volume of *National Geographic*, I began thumbing through the articles, studying the pictures and imagining those far-away places. Another crash. Several more books were scattered on the floor behind me. I peeked through the stacks. No one was in the adjacent aisle. At that moment, Miss Ellis, the night librarian, walked down the aisle in short, quick steps, her lips pursed.

"Young man, you are going to have to stop fooling around back here or I'm going to have to ask you to leave."

"Miss Ellis, I didn't do that," I said, embarrassed at the accusation.

She didn't know my name. "Young man, you are the only person in these stacks."

I was speechless, and there was no use arguing with her. She turned to walk away, and she hadn't taken more than two of her quick, banty-rooster steps when the top two shelves of books in one section began to fall out, like water over the edge of a cliff. They didn't pop out all at once. They fell out a few at a time like they were being pushed out. Miss Ellis wheeled around, fire in her eyes, her mouth screwed up like she was sucking on a lemon.

"Pick those up, right now. No, you come with me right now."

I was led to the front desk where she took my card, and, after telling me that my parents would be notified, ordered me to leave. Which I did.

Embarrassed, I walked through the parking lot, not believing what had happened. I opened my door, then shut it and went around to the other side to let Catie in. I stood there, holding the door. The events of the night struck me suddenly. I was outside myself looking at myself, and what I saw was funny. Opening the door for a ghost. A ghost who had knocked books off a shelf to get me in trouble. I began to laugh, and I laughed and giggled uncontrollably. This was fun. She was fun. And I liked her so much. I think I felt her laughing with me as we drove home.

B eth called the stock tank behind our house her "wonder place" because it was her favorite place to sit and wonder about things. Even better than the garden.

The tank was located about a hundred yards west of the bois d'arc tree. Its dam blocked the drainage between two small swells in the land. When full, the tank was maybe forty yards long and twenty yards wide. But during the drought, which had been there from the time we first moved to the country, it was rarely full.

Beth spent hours there, sometimes fishing, sometimes tossing rocks or wading, but usually just sitting around thinking. She had theories about everything. Air, she told me once, consisted of "pieces," and the piece that came from the north and hit our faces was the same piece that had started traveling south from up in Alaska. It had somehow managed to cross the Canadian Rockies and rush down the Alberta and Montana plains. Sometimes the piece traveled through Yellowstone Park, and sometimes it went east of there. Beth had the rest of the journey mapped out. She said it made the wind that touched her "special." Beth also had a theory about wind and smell. It was her conclusion that if a person's sense of smell was working properly, he or she could determine where a piece of air had passed. She claimed that on some days she could pick up the scent of the salt water in the Gulf of Mexico. Other times, she was certain the bluebonnets were blooming in central Texas. She could smell them, she said.

On dark, calm nights, the stars were mirrored in the still water of the tank. Beth would sit on the hill above the water and count the stars that were reflected beneath her. One night she dashed into my room yelling at me to hurry to the pond. She had something special to show me. I went with her. There, on a moonless night, in the perfectly motionless water, the Milky Way was faintly reflected. Nothing could have excited Beth more than that sight.

Beth's perception and powers of observation worried me. I was almost certain she was watching me and wondering what I was doing. And my worries were warranted.

One afternoon in December of 1955, Beth and I were sitting in the short, dry grass near the edge of the water. I remember the day as one of those frequent, balmy days that occur in North Texas in December. In the afternoons, even a jacket was unnecessary.

Beth was talking. "Mr. Isbell keeps telling me there're catfish here."

"Uh huh."

"He says they're down in that thin mud that your feet touch just after you go through the cold current. You know, down in that stuff you get to before you touch the hard bottom."

"Uh huh," I answered again drowsily.

"He says he used to fish down here with Catie Waldrop."

I woke up quickly.

Beth continued. "Catie Waldrop was a little girl who used to live in our house. Mr. and Mrs. Isbell told me all about her. Said I would have really liked her."

I relaxed a little.

Beth said, "Catie Waldrop died when she was only fourteen. That's real sad, isn't it?"

"Yeah."

"Mrs. Isbell almost cries when she talks about her."

"I know. She's told me about her."

"Did she show you some pictures of Catie?"

"Yeah."

"I saw some, too. She was so pretty. She would have been a nice friend."

"I know."

"Just think, if she were living now, she would be thirty-one or thirty-two. Now, she'll be fourteen forever."

I didn't respond.

There were a few moments of silence, then Beth asked me, "Billy, what were you doing the other night when you opened the car door on the other side from the driver? I saw you, you know."

"I know."

"Well, what?"

I thought quickly and answered, "I was just fooling around. You know, Dad said I had to open the door for girls."

"So, you were just practicing?"

"Yeah." I breathed a little easier.

"Billy, I've been watching you a lot."

"What do you mean?" This was getting dangerous, I thought.

"I'm not a little girl anymore. I *am* twelve years old."

I wanted to say, "Just because Mother bought you a bra, you think you're a woman." Instead, I said to her,

"I don't know what you're talking about."

"You just seem to wander around here a lot. You're always going out to that big tree in the field. I saw you put things in that hole in the trunk."

"It was just a note for Earnie."

"I looked, but I didn't see anything."

"That's 'cause he got it."

"You go down to the creek a lot at night, too."

"What's wrong with that?"

"I dunno. It's just strange being out in the dark like that. Don't you get scared?"

"No, nighttime's just like day 'cept it's dark."

"I guess so. You know, Mr. Isbell said Catie Waldrop used to go down to the creek, even at night."

"So?"

"Well, if she went, then it's not so strange that you go. Mr. Isbell said he went down there one night 'cause they were worried about her."

"What happened?"

"She was all right. She was down there on that spit of sand above the pool where the fish run in the spring. She had a fire going and was sitting beside it. Said she was okay, just thinking about things."

I could picture Catie, sitting cross-legged before a small fire, watching the flames, thinking maybe about something nice or even about something sad that had happened. She might have been wondering about what life would be like when she grew up. I remember even now the terrible ache I got just thinking about her there beside the fire.

Beth took me away from those thoughts. "Billy, you go down on the creek and see Hebronetta Sikes, don't you?"

"Yeah, sometimes."

"What's she like?"

I described her, omitting, of course, her helping me find Catie. I did, however, tell Beth about some of Hebronetta's ghost stories.

"Would you take me with you sometime?" Beth asked.

"Sure, Hebronetta would like to meet you."

I was relieved. Beth was perceptive, but she had made no connection between me and Catie.

It was a dreary, bleak day when I took Beth to meet Hebronetta. The balmy days of early December had disappeared. The wind was now out of the north, ice cold and blustery. Sleet followed by a few flakes of snow fell out of the gray sky.

Beth and I bundled up and walked fast. She was apprehensive, probably because of the stories she had heard about Hebronetta. By the time we reached the trail that led up the draw to the cabin, Beth was completely silent. We trudged along, hugging ourselves to keep warm. When we reached the clearing, there ahead of us was Hebronetta, standing statue-like by the trail. She was wearing a man's dress hat and a knee-length gray overcoat. Smoke poured out of the pipe she was smoking. She looked like a spy, waiting for important information.

I had told Hebronetta that Beth was coming, but I didn't expect her visit to be such a big event. It was. Hebronetta had decorated several small trees and bushes that grew scattered in the meadow.

Hebronetta looked at Beth with a pleasantness that broke into a broad smile as we got closer. I might as well have been on the other side of the moon that afternoon. Hebronetta, her smile exuding affection, held out her arms and, looking only at my sister, said: "I's so happy yous come to see me, Beth. Not offen I has people down here, much less female people."

I said, "Beth, this is Hebronetta."

They stood, staring at each other, Beth caught up in Hebronetta's affection but still awed by this woman whose reputation was such that one doubted whether she really existed.

"I fixed up de place for you all. You gots to come at night to see de whole show, though."

I looked around. The trees were covered with hundreds of ornaments. The most impressive and the most numerous were made of tinfoil shaped into little frames that surrounded tiny mirrors. There were also some store-bought, round glass ornaments of many colors. Popcorn strings, some obviously already partly eaten by the birds, wrapped around the trees. Icicles were draped over each branch. Beneath the trees were white sheets, and encircling each trunk was cardboard about a foot or so high. Inside the cardboard wall were lanterns.

Beth stood, fascinated. She looked down at the sheets and asked, "What's the yellow stuff?"

"Oh, dats de dog pee. You know how de dogs are."

We all laughed. Then we went inside, and I sat around drinking hot chocolate and eating popcorn while Hebronetta showed Beth every nook and cranny of the cabin.

Later they left, and I spent the next hour browsing around, looking at the pictures on the wall until distant voices reminded me I wasn't in a football stadium. Hebronetta and Beth, both talking at the same time, drew closer to the cabin. I heard Beth say, " . . . and that's why I think that the blue jay is kin to the oak tree." I had not heard that particular one before, but it was obviously one of Beth's theories on kinship.

I asked them what they were taking about. Beth said, "It's a secret just between me and Hebronetta."

Hebronetta glanced over at me. Her mouth opened. Her left eyebrow arched upward. Her right eye closed in a big wink. She said, "Beth and I has secrets, jes' like you an' me has secrets."

Once again, I knew I was safe.

Even though I was in love with Catie and she occupied most of my thoughts, other things did happen to me. I played ball and of course I went to school. During the '55-'56 school year, my ninth grade year, Gary was probably my best friend. Both he and I were good students, but put us together at school, and there would be trouble, the consequences of which we usually managed to escape. At least we did until just a couple of weeks prior to the Christmas holidays. I still remember quite well how we got caught.

It all began one morning before school. Gary and I met at our usual loitering spot, which was beside the tennis courts, just at the top of the terraced rock gardens. Gary was there before I got off the bus. As I was approaching him, I could tell by his discreet motions towards me that, whatever he had in mind, it was to be a secret. Like a spy in the movies, he nodded toward his right hand, and when I looked, he cupped it, disclosing a cherry bomb, that mammoth, soon-to-be-outlawed firecracker. I asked him what he was going to do with it, and he said, "Whadda ya think, stupid, I'm gonna light it." When I asked where, he told me in music class when Mr. Beeson wasn't looking. He said he needed my help. I thought he was crazy and said so. He must have agreed with me, because he then suggested we get Wanton to do it. Gary, like me, was friendly to Wanton, and Wanton responded to him as he did to me. I thought that using Wanton was a much better idea than using me, so, after very little hesitation, I said I was in. We yelled at Wanton, who was lurking down on the football field.

He ambled up to where we were, and when he heard the plan, he immediately and happily agreed to light the firecracker. He said he already had matches and a cigarette lighter.

I didn't walk into school very happy that morning. I kept looking at Wanton, who beamed through the veneer of grime that covered his face. I knew that what I had done was not right. But, not for the first time, or the last, my conscience was not strong enough to cause me to rescind what I had already planned.

Music class, which met at one o'clock, normally lasted only half an hour, but that December, the ninth graders were taking time from another period and practicing for an hour and a half each day. The entire ninth grade was singing *The Nutcracker Suite* using lyrics a college student had written. With the day of the program fast approaching, Mr. Beeson, the teacher, was even more anxious than he had been the rest of the year, which meant he was on the verge of a nervous breakdown. During the preceding days, the wrinkles on his forehead had increased in number and in depth, and, at crucial points during practice, the veins in his skinny neck looked as if they would rupture at any moment. Mr. Beeson was also more brutal than usual this time of year, which was particularly dangerous to the boys and embarrassing to the girls. As we sang, he would march back and forth in front of us, stopping before each person to determine if he or she was singing "breathy." He would hold his palm within inches of our mouths, and if he felt any breath coming from a boy, he would double his fist and pop him with his knuckles, just above the hairline. Several of us usually had chronic sore heads, particularly during concert times. If a girl sang "breathy," she received only a slight slap on the face. The following year, one of those slaps cost Mr. Beeson his job and resulted in our town losing not only a music teacher but two star athletes who moved away with their dad. It was ironic that Mr. Beeson, that nervous, little chain-smoking music teacher, had twin sons in high school who were unquestionably the town's star athletes.

On the day of the bomb, Mr. Beeson was as tense as I had ever seen him, mainly because the performance was only two days away. The entire class was in front of him on risers set on the stage. Gary, Wanton and I were on the top row. Wanton, towering above the others, was at one end. Gary and I were at the opposite end. Wanton even being there was unusual. He seldom sang with the group, since his main job was to cut hundreds of sheets of white notebook paper into little pieces. On the night of the performance, Wanton and two others were to climb high above the stage, and during the final song, they were to shovel out boxes of the confetti-like paper which would float down, like snow, upon the singers. Mr. Beeson said the effect would be beautiful, but we were worried about someone the size of Wanton crouching on a beam twenty-five feet above us.

Halfway through the period, while we were singing "The Waltz of the Flowers" for the third time, Mr. Beeson turned around to pick up some sheet music. At the exact moment his eyes looked away, I saw Wanton turn his upper body to the right. In his left hand was the cherry bomb. In his right hand was the lighter. I saw the sparks and had only a split second to stick my fingers in my ears and squeeze my eyes shut. Even though I got my ears covered, the sound of the explosion almost knocked me over. I slid down on the risers hoping they wouldn't collapse as the other kids screamed and stampeded off the stage and out the door. I sat there with my palms over my eyes and my fingers still in my ears. It seemed like forever before the room was cleared of people. It became very quiet as the scent of the burned powder settled over the risers. Slowly, I removed my hands, opened my eyes and looked around. Through the blue haze, I could see Gary and Wanton sitting on the risers, their eyes still shut tightly and their fingers still in their ears. Standing, facing the three of us, was Mr. Beeson, glowering with the most savage and murderous look I had seen or will probably ever see on a human face. He just stood there, frozen. Only his eyes moved. Slowly they went from one of us to the other. When his voice finally escaped from his contorted mouth, he said he didn't know which one of us did it, but he knew we were all three involved in the most despicable act he had ever witnessed in a classroom. Looking straight at me, he said he could prove it, because we were the only ones prepared to keep out the noise. After he spoke, he became silent and still, and he glared at us. It seemed as if I had reached the hell the preachers talked about, and it would never end. But it did. Mr. Beeson motioned us out the door, and he marched us in a direct line to the principal's office. The silent crowds of students stepped back against the lockers and let us through. They were stunned. None of them had ever seen an execution.

My only hope of salvation was with Mr. Evans, the principal. He was a strong, quiet, mild-mannered man who did not advocate corporal punishment. He relied instead on his powers of persuasion, his ability to make a student feel guilty about what he had done. In really tough situations, Mr. Evans used letters and phone calls to parents.

I soon found out that Mr. Evans was out of the office that day. Taking his place was Mr. Norton. Mr. Norton had quit coaching football because of criticism that he was too tough on the players. Unlike Mr. Evans, Mr. Norton not only believed in the power of bodily punishment, but he also did not know there was any other way to deal with a discipline problem, no matter how minor the offense.

Mr. Beeson opened the door for us, and followed us in to the little room where Mr. Norton sat with his new burr haircut and a slight smile that would have made Adolf Hitler look like a saint.

He looked carefully at each of us and said, "Well, Mr. Beeson, it looks like we have a problem today doesn't it?"

"Yes, sir, it does, Mr. Norton," Beeson answered. "These young animals have committed the most outrageous act of conduct this school has ever seen. I haven't even been out in the halls to find out how many of our children have been severely injured by these three monsters."

Mr. Norton sat unmoving in his chair, and listened as Mr. Beeson described what sounded like a German attack on London. When Mr. Beeson began to sob, Mr. Norton slightly tilted his head toward us, just enough to make his demonic smile penetrate to our bones. Sweat was forming on his upper lip and at the top of his forehead. He ran his tongue over his upper lip three or four times. I could see that he was formulating a plan.

Both men became silent. The only sound in the room was the loud tick-tocking of the clock on the wall behind Mr. Norton. Wanton, Gary and I stood almost motionless, moving only to look down at the floor so we could escape the glares that seemed unending. Mr. Norton broke the spell. He said that before he reported the matter to our parents, he was going to punish us in such a way that, for the rest of our lives, whenever we heard the name "Norton," we would quiver in fear. He paused, tapping his index finger on the side of his nose, then announced the punishment. Gary was to give Wanton three licks with the board. Wanton was to then hit me three times. I was to finish the round by busting Gary. The board was an inch thick. Holes had been drilled in it so the air would not slow it down when it was swung. Mr. Norton, his face still frozen in the sadistic smile, handed the instrument to Gary. He told Wanton to bend over and place his hands on the desk. Wanton managed a wink and a half grin as he complied. Mr. Norton warned us that the licks had better be tough or he would double them and do the job himself. We all stood there waiting. Gary hesitated, then brought the wooden board far back and swung at Wanton. I felt myself become sick as I saw Wanton's face turn so white that the dirt disappeared. His cheeks bulged, and his eyes watered. I could almost feel his butt breaking. The second and third licks were just as terrible, and when my turn came, I didn't think I would be alive when Wanton hit me. I would die before the blows struck. Then Mr. Norton would feel terrible. There would be a big funeral at the First Baptist Church. My church would be too small to hold the thousands of people who would be there feeling so sorry for my family and for me and hating Mr. Norton for what he had made Wanton do. My dad and mom would be in the front row, sobbing. All my friends would be crying uncontrollably. While they were burying me, the police would be talking to Mr. Norton, who would be praying he was going to prison so he could escape being lynched by the mobs of people that would be gathered on the front steps of the police station.

I closed my eyes and waited. And waited. When the blow came, it was nothing more than a firm pat. I could hear Mr. Norton yelling at Wanton, telling him he still had three to go and that if he didn't do it right, he was going to make Gary's licks look like a back rub compared to what he was going to do. I squeezed my eyes even tighter. I heard Wanton say he couldn't do it. Mr. Norton screamed he would, and Wanton said like hell he would. I didn't look around or move until Mr. Norton grabbed my arm and shoved me into a chair. He made Wanton get back in the whipping position. He hit Wanton so hard that water shot out of his eyes. Even Mr. Beeson gulped. Wanton stood up, bit his lower lip and walked out the door. He missed the Christmas program

141

and never came back to school until after the holidays. Gary and I never got our licks.

My parents punished me, but not as severely as I had expected. They wouldn't allow me to go to the Christmas dance at school. I had looked forward to going, but not to making the choice of whom to take. Susan Morrison wanted me to take her. At least that's what some of her friends told me, but I was just too much in love with Catie to ask anyone else. I would have felt terrible knowing that Catie was somewhere out along that creek and not with me. What I had initially planned to do was to go by myself. Most of the kids went to dances without dates anyway, so I wouldn't have been conspicuous going without a girlfriend. Then I could have asked Catie to go with me.

I told Catie about what had happened at school with Wanton, Gary and me. Instead of sitting on the rock and talking to her, I had taken a walk. I went to the creek before dark, knowing Catie would meet me, and as usual, I felt her presence strongly. She was so real that, as I walked through the field, I looked down several times to see if her steps were making indentations in the grass. Of course, they weren't.

"Can you imagine how bad Wanton feels tonight? . . . He'd feel worse if he knew that Gary and me got off without anything. I just don't understand why some people have so many things happen good and others have so many things happen bad. You oughta see where Wanton lives. It's a part of town right at the south edge, you know, south of the school. All that's there are little wooden shacks and lots of dogs. The streets aren't even paved. And it's called 'Heaven's Acres.' My dad said the name must have been someone's idea of a cruel joke, or maybe they named it that way because those people who live there will get the first shot at heaven. . . .

"I guess you've wondered why life can be so unfair, haven't you, Catie? . . . Lots of times, I've felt real bad about your dying. That doesn't seem right either. . . . And then I had to be the cause of it. Not your dying. I mean Wanton's getting into trouble." I wondered if Catie knew the answers to all these questions I was beginning to have as I grew older. There were so many things I wanted to ask her, but I never did. Even when I finally got the chance, I forgot to ask, and still, after all these years, I've never found satisfactory answers.

J ust before Christmas, Mr. Isbell, my dad and I were in our kitchen. Mr. Isbell was standing by the sink, leaning forward, looking out toward the driveway.

"Bill, I can't believe you're finally going to put a goal up for Billy. The season's been going for almost two months now."

My dad responded, "I have been a little neglectful. He'll make up for it quickly, though."

"Well, you'd better do it in a hurry. If the wind doesn't get hung up on some barbed wire fence, it's fixin' to get cold real soon." Mr. Isbell pointed outside, "You know, a good place for it would be right over there." Dad got up and went to the window. Mr. Isbell continued, "Little girl who used to live here had a goal out there, and it was a pretty good place."

"Was that Catie Waldrop?" I asked.

"Yep," said Mr. Isbell.

"Was she a good basketball player?"

"Catie could play any sport well. I doubt if there were many boys who could outrun her. She could throw a softball a mile and hit one 'bout as far. She was always picked first at church and school stuff. Basketball was probably her best sport, though. Too bad they didn't have a girl's team, 'cause she would have been really something. She could take the ball away from anyone. You had to be some kind of dribbler to get around her."

"Is that the little girl who died?" asked Dad.

"Yes."

"That's sad," said Dad.

I walked out of the kitchen and went upstairs to my room. I opened the drawer and pulled out a picture of Catie that I had carefully hidden. For a long time I stood there looking at her. Then I went outside and walked up the driveway until I found where the goal had been. I had never noticed it before. I kicked around at the bits of old concrete and thought about Catie, dribbling and shooting . . . and laughing.

With Mr. Isbell's prodding, Dad had the goal up in a short time. I swept the large gravel away so that I had a fairly smooth court to play on. Coach Chambers had told me I needed to do a lot of practicing during the holidays since I was 12th man on a 12-man team that had won only one game. Our team had lost several games by large scores, the most embarrassing one being to Central Junior High in a tournament. They had scored the first 21 points, then kept pouring it on. The final score had been 73–24. Coach told me I had made a great contribution to their victory. In four minutes, I was able to foul three times, miss four shots, and allow the other team to steal the ball from me three times, each of which was converted into an easy layup. No one knew better than I that I had to improve my ball-handling skills. Having my own goal would help a lot.

Within a few days I felt I was improving. I spent hours dribbling with my left hand and switching my dribble from my right to my left hand and then from my left to my right hand.

Every time I played, I fantasized I was winning the big games. With every bounce of the ball, part of the world around me would be obliterated. The pastures in

146

front of me would disappear, as would the barn and the house. They would be replaced in my mind by a jam-packed gymnasium. I would be whisked away from the driveway goal to a court surrounded by a huge crowd of fans:

My team was trailing by almost twenty points early in the 4th quarter. I had been out with a cut on my chin, and although it was still bleeding some, the coach had to have me back in the game or the championship would be lost. The crowd stood up and screamed when I walked to the scorer's table. I nodded toward the cheerleaders to let them know that I could make it even with my injury. They acknowledged my nod with worried, pleading looks that told me to be careful. Within seconds I had the ball in my hands, and I knew exactly where to go with it. Weaving in and out of the defensive players, I made my way with lightning-fast speed down the court. Just at the edge of the free throw line, I came to a sudden stop and jumped straight up, releasing the ball at the top of my jump. Nothing but net! Time and time again, I did the same thing, sometimes going to my right, sometimes going to my left. The crowd was in a frenzy as we narrowed the score. We finally got within one point. We had the ball out. Fifteen seconds were left on the clock. Every single person in the packed gym knew that I would take the final shot. The cheerleaders were on their knees, their hands over their faces, praying that I would make the basket. I took the ball on the out-of-bounds throw and started down the court. At mid-court, I made

*a quick move to my left, then came back to my right with
such a crossover dribble that I got that one step I needed
to get free. I headed straight toward the tip of the circle.
There was an eerie silence in the gym. Just as I reached
the circle . . .*

"Billy, it's time to eat. Wash up," Mother called.
The magic was gone.

Catie showed up one day while I was playing basketball. Although I didn't actually see her, I know she was
there because of what happened that day and because
she later told me she did, laughing the whole time.

It was two days before Christmas. The cold, gray
sleety weather we'd had when I had taken Beth to meet
Hebronetta had gone wherever weather goes, and its
replacement was the kind of day we usually got in North
Texas at Christmas time. It was almost spring-like. The
air was dry, and the blue of the sky was broken only by
white strands of a few high cirrus clouds.

I was shooting baskets with an audience of one,
Beth. "Do you really think all this playing will make you
better?" she asked.

"It sure won't make me worse," I answered, as the
ball missed the basket and hit the backboard.

"That's true."

A little perturbed, I said, "Why don't you quit
standing around and play some yourself? It wouldn't
hurt you either."

Soon it was two playing with no one watching. Beth had been lately moving away from her nonathletic life. She had even thrown the ball at the basket a few times. I passed the ball to her, and she ran toward the basket and heaved the ball toward the rim, missing everything. For the next half hour, I tried to teach her how to shoot. I could tell her future was not in basketball. After shooting practice, I showed her some of my dribbling moves. She wasn't impressed. "I bet I could take the ball away just like that Central boy did," Beth chided.

"You're welcome to try," I answered.

We set up about twenty feet from the goal. I was in the correct position. Beth was just standing in front of me with no idea what to do. I went first one way, then the other. Then I dribbled back out to where we had started. Beth just ran after me, squealing. I started a drive directly to the basket. I passed Beth. The ball was gone. It wasn't there when my hand came down on it. It was rolling northward, into the pasture.

Beth taunted me, "Good job, Billy."

"You didn't do that."

"Try it again," she said. "We'll see if it's luck."

Again and again I tried to reach the basket. No matter what I did, I would lose the ball. Once, as I just stood there with the ball in both hands, it was slapped away from me. And Beth didn't do it. Her eyes got big. "How did that happen?"

"Beats me," I said. But I knew.

After Beth left, I walked out toward the creek. I really chewed Catie out for embarrassing me in front of my little sister.

Even now, when I think of Christmas, I think of the Isbells' home that Christmas Eve afternoon in 1955 when they had a party for neighbors and a few people from town. The day was not very cold, well above the temperature required for a white Christmas. But it was cool enough for an enormous fire, and huge oak logs burned in the fireplace. The mantel and a couple of the table tops were covered with cotton, which served as snow beneath little Christmas villages. Red ribbons and green mistletoe were everywhere in the white rooms. The big Christmas tree was in the living room, but the kitchen, the entrance hall, and the porch also had brightly lit trees.

When we walked in the front door, the first person I saw was Hebronetta, who gave me a big smile and wink. She was sitting in a big white chair, laughing and talking with Earnie Wayne's dad. Hebronetta had on the darndest outfit I had ever seen. She wore a gray sweatshirt with sequins sewed all over it. Her skirt was long and black, but it didn't cover the old black boots that she always wore when she wasn't wearing her tennis shoes. She was wearing both a gold-looking necklace and a pearl necklace, and hanging from her ears were earrings in the shape of flamingos. Her lips were painted with the reddest lipstick I had ever seen.

I chuckled to myself when I looked at Earnie Wayne. He was a carbon copy of his dad.

I was surprised to see two of my teachers, Mrs. Pettit and Miss Langford. Mrs. Pettit taught algebra and taught it tough. Her competence and demeanor deterred any misbehavior in her classes. One would rather face Mr. Norton's paddle than Mrs. Pettit's disdain. Miss Langford taught history and was what we called in those days an "old maid." She was a wonderful old, gruff lady who had once been principal of a boys' school in New Orleans. Besides being famous for her tough exams and pulling the ears of misbehaving students, she was well known for her hugs. She had given me one after the incident with the firecracker. The hug didn't tell me that what I had done was okay, but it told me the world was not going to end, at least not that afternoon.

Earnie Wayne and I hung around together that night, mostly drifting from the fireplace to the punch bowl and cookie trays, passing among the animated conversations of the adults. The kids had one punch bowl. The adults had another one.

Around six o'clock, just before the party was over, Mr. Isbell announced that he was going to take a picture of the guests. He said he and Mrs. Isbell had been having this party for twenty-five years, and each year they took a picture of the group. Every year, a week before Christmas, they placed all the photographs on the dining room table to remind them of the many wonderful friends they had made over the years.

I knew who would be in those pictures, so I almost went crazy waiting for Mr. Isbell to finish. After the last shot, I went quickly to the dining room. In a circle, facing outward on the large table were twenty-four photographs in wooden frames. Under each was the date. I slowly walked around looking for 1937. I found

151

it. Ten people were in the picture. Catie was on the front row, smiling as usual. In the 1936 picture, she looked a lot younger. Like Beth. She had no figure. But she was smiling and had freckles. Her mother smiled just like she did. Until then I had never even thought about what a pretty woman her mother had been.

No one else was in the room, so I sat down and looked at Catie for a long time. Then I went outside and walked around the house talking to her, hoping she was there to hear me. I left the door open for her when I came back inside.

It was early, but it was dark when we returned home that Christmas Eve. Texas had no winter daylight savings time in those days, so, in late December, 6:30 was way into the night.

After a few minutes inside, I left the house and walked to the road where I stood for awhile looking at our Christmas tree, with all its colored lights, shining through the front window. From there I walked up the driveway, then decided to continue on toward the back pasture. I wasn't going anywhere in particular. Just wandering around thinking, mostly about Christmas and Catie. I was trying to imagine what she was thinking as she drifted around that night. I assumed then that Catie just floated around most of the time, unless she was with me. I thought it must have been particularly difficult for her to look through windows and see Christmas trees and presents and log fires and people celebrating.

I heard footsteps behind me. It was Beth.

"Can I walk with you?" she asked.

"Sure," I said, and really meant it.

We moved quietly over the pasture toward the rim overlooking the creek. Once we stopped and looked back. The house had grown small. Its lights were the only ones breaking the darkness. Even the glow from town was subdued.

"Look up," I told Beth. Above us were millions of stars. The Milky Way was even brighter than the night Beth and I had seen it reflected in the stock tank.

"You know," said Beth, "it's like I've never seen it before. I think I can see the stars in three dimensions tonight. I know it should be impossible, their being so far away, but I think I can see depth out there."

"Yeah, it does seem that way. Look up there at the Northern Cross. Did you know that at Christmas time, it sits upright in the sky?"

"Uh huh, and do you know what else it's called?"

"No, what?" I asked.

"Cygnus the Swan."

I told Beth, "In history class, Miss Langford talked about 'prairie nights.' We all kind of laughed about it, but I know now what she was talking about. She said there was nothing as fantastic as the prairie at night back when the first settlers traveled across the Great Plains. There was no light anywhere to interfere with the stars once a person got away from the campfires. One day, Miss Langford quoted Francis Parkman talking about the moon rising from the black outline of the prairie. I wish I could remember it. Something about the light of the moon pouring over the rim, and a terrible howl going up from some animal, a wolf, I guess. Anyway she made it sound real and kinda scary when she read it. Just like I was there."

"Who's Francis Parkman?"

"He was a historian who took a trip along the Oregon Trail sometime in the 1840s. He wrote about it and named the book *The Oregon Trail*.

"Would I like it?"

"I dunno. Mother and Dad have a copy. Ask them."

After a few moments of silence, Beth said, "Billy, I've got a secret."

"What's that?"

"Follow me."

"Where?"

"Just follow me."

Instead of going up and then down to the creek, we turned west and stumbled and walked up and down parallel to the creek but out of sight of it. Finally, Beth told me her secret was just up ahead.

"Okay, duck and get down low." I did.

We crawled up the back side of a hill. Suddenly we reached the top. The land below dropped away.

"My gosh," we both said simultaneously. Below us were lights that looked like stars that had fallen on the ground. They were flickering.

"That's Hebronetta's place," I said.

"You're right. And we're in the place where she likes to watch the moon come through. She calls it the Moon Gap."

"I know."

Not speaking, we lay there on our stomachs for a long time, our chins propped up with our hands. We watched the pulsating light from the little lanterns far below us. Then we turned over and lay on our backs and looked upward, mesmerized by the millions of miles of magic above us. I knew Catie was there with us looking at the same sky, and I almost told Beth. But I never could, and I remained quiet.

Beth finally spoke, "I wonder who Hebronetta really is?"

"I don't know. I don't know," I said.

Later that night, after sitting in front of the tree with Mother and Dad and Beth, I went to my room. I opened a drawer in my desk. At the back were several paperback books, which I removed. Behind them was a small Christmas present. The wrapping was red and the ribbon green. I pulled it out and read the card attached to it. It said, "Merry Christmas to Catie from Billy." I had wanted to say "love," but I was still a little embarrassed by having written "I love you" on the note I'd placed in the tree.

The gift was a small bottle of Shalimar perfume like the kind Gary had bought for Mary Jane. I took it with me out to the tree and placed it in the hole. Hoping Catie was nearby, I said to the darkness, "Merry Christmas, Catie. You'll like this. It smells real good. . . . We leave our Christmas tree lights on all night tonight. Be sure to look at them. They're real pretty."

I walked away thinking more about what I had given Catie than what was under the tree for me to open the next morning. I thought about Gary telling me that Mary Jane had cried when he gave her the perfume. I hoped Catie would cry when she opened her present. It would mean she liked me a lot.

The pot-bellied stove threw out enough heat to hold back the cold that seeped into the cabin from the raw January night outside. The soft crackling of the burning wood made a duet with the whistling of the wind as it found its way through tiny cracks in the walls and by the windows. Hebronetta got up from her chair often to peek out the window. "'Fraid it too cold an' windy to snow tonight, Billy. For snow to hit here, it have to start comin' down somewhere in Oklahoma, dat win's so hard."

"That's silly, Hebronetta. That's what a blizzard is. Wind and snow."

"Well, I don' know 'bout dat. All I know is, it look like snow up dere, an' de wind is blowin' sumpin' terrible, an it's cold as I can ever 'member, and it ain't snowin', so I says it's too cold and windy."

"You're impossible to argue with, Hebronetta."

"I is right on dis," she said as she took one more peek. "God wouldn't get out on a night like dis."

"I did."

"Yeah, an' dat proves you ain't as smart as God."

Hebronetta hunched over in the chair and bent closer to the fire. Suddenly she sat straight up with a jerk. It scared me.

"What's wrong?"

"Oh, nuttin'." She breathed a deep breath. Sweat broke out on her forehead. "I guess I's jes' gettin' old. Das all."

"You're not that old."

"Oh, but I is, Billy boy. I wuz jes' thinkin' dis afternoon 'bout how many Januarys I seen an' how many winters I's watched turn into spring. Jes' think, another football season has come an' gone. Everthang does. Everthang has its time, an' so do I. Like it say in Cleesiastees in de Bible. Dere's a time to put on de uniform an' a time to take it off."

"It doesn't say that, Hebronetta."

"Oh yes it do. Dere's a time to laugh an' a time to cry. Dere's a time to plant yo' seed an' a time to pick de crop dat grow from de seed. Dere's a time to live an' a time to die. A time to fish an' a time to hunt. Dere's a time to play football an' a time to play basketball an' a time to play baseball."

"Where did you learn all that?"

"It's in de Bible. Right dere. God, he smart. He knowed what he was doin'. Jes' think how he 'ranged things. What if he had put baseball in de winter? But he didn't. An' he didn't put basketball or football in de summer. No, God, he smart. He put dem in de right time of de year. An' he put me in at de right time an' he'll take me at de right time. I still think he take my boy at de wrong time, though."

"You never told me you had a boy."

"Homer Winslow Sikes, Jr. He a real good boy. Got hisself kilt in de Argonne Forest over dere. He still dere. De people, dey takes care of his grave. Dey used to write me an' send me pitchers of where he buried. Now dey grandchirin takes care of his grave. Junior, he was a good boy."

All I could say was that I was sorry. Then I sat quietly for a time, letting Hebronetta think.

She wasn't quiet for long. She wanted to talk. "De days, dey gettin' hard, Billy. Dey used to be so easy an' so long an' so much fun. It seem like forever dat you grows up. De days an' de months an' de years dey jes' stretch out so much dat de time, it don't move atall. Mos' peoples, dey stops stretchin' de days when dey gets a certain age, an' when dey do dat, dey life, it start speeding up an' dey gets old. I's kept dem days as long as I could, an' I thinks I gots de secret to makin' de long life."

"What's that?" I asked.

"It's in de seein', in de lookin' at thangs. You gots it. Beth, she gots it even more. Dat sister of yours, she can see de whole world, both de inside an' de outside. She look at a flower, she don't jes' see pretty colors. No, she see right through de flower an' sees everthang, people, animals, what makes de world work. We's lucky. We's got lots of people 'round here dat stretch out de days, 'cause dey sees it all. An' dat includes seein' people. Takes a lot more time when you lookin' an' studyin' and thinkin' 'bout thangs, then when you jes' sittin' 'roun' worryin' 'bout de next day and whether you feels perfect or not. Mr. an' Missus Isbell, dey don't let a sunset drop down over de edge without dey seein' it, an' dey up in de morning to watch de sun climb up from de other side of de worl'. Dey sees other people, too, like you and me. Now you worries 'bout your Catie, but I knows she lived a long life even though she passed when she only fourteen. I can tell dat she stretched dose days. You know, Billy, dere's sumpin' magic-like 'bout dis place, de creek, de farms, de fields, de grass. Dere's sumpin' here dat make us see all de world 'round us. Now all of us, we human, but we still like de flowers an' de trees an' de animals. Dey gots so much time, an' we only gots so much time, an' no matter how much we pulls it out, it gots to end sometime. An' I beginning to see de end of my time."

Hebronetta put her hand to her chest and breathed in deeply. I couldn't get her to admit that anything was wrong, and in a minute or so she seemed all right. We talked for another hour, and I did much of the talking. I told her about school and how well I was liking it. She laughed a lot as she listened to me tell about our basketball team. We had finally won our second game, against one of the best teams in the area. What we didn't know at the time of the game was that their best six players were out with the flu. The second time we played them, they beat us 81-33.

The stove kept us warm while I talked of Catie. I told about taking her to the movies downtown. Once, I (we) had gone with another couple, and I felt kinda stupid sitting with a space between them and me. Many times I felt stupid about what was happening, but I felt sad and frustrated even more than I felt stupid. It hurt to listen to other guys talk about kissing their girlfriends, and it hurt to see boys and girls holding hands at school or at the movies. Hebronetta thought my romance with Catie was hopeless. I was beginning to agree, but I was still optimistic that at some time, she would become a real girl. If she was just a vapor, then how could she write with a pencil or push books off a shelf or take a basketball from me? And how did the faint scent of perfume reach me when Catie was around, unless there really was some substance to her? Except in a movie or two, I had never heard of anything ever happening that was in any way similar to what was happening to me. Even Hebronetta, with all her experience with ghosts, had only observed them, not communicated with one as I had.

As bitterly cold as it was that January night in 1956, I didn't feel it at all as I walked home. I was completely absorbed with thoughts of Catie.

The doorbell rang. I was on the floor in the living room reading the spread-out newspaper. Someone else answered, and no one called me, so I continued studying the sports page, paying little attention to the soft voices that came from the foyer, then faded as the speakers went toward another room.

Mother broke my concentration when she asked me to come to the dining room. I responded like any fourteen-year-old boy. Slowly. When I got there, she and Dad were standing beside the Isbells, and I knew when I saw them that something was wrong. Mother and Dad looked sad; the Isbells were distraught.

"Billy, I'm afraid we have some real bad news," my mother said.

"What?" I asked, afraid of the answer.

"Hebronetta Sikes passed away this afternoon."

Mother wasn't telling the truth. Hebronetta was alive. She was talking. She was laughing. She was moving around. She couldn't be erased forever.

"What happened?" I asked.

Mr. Isbell told me that about noon, Hebronetta had called Mrs. Ingram and told her she was real sick. She said her chest and arms were hurting, and she couldn't breathe. Mrs. Ingram called Mr. Isbell, and he called an ambulance. Then he and Mrs. Isbell ran down to the cabin, but by the time they reached it, it was too late. He said Hebronetta was in bed, and she looked very peaceful, like she had stopped hurting before she died. Mr. Isbell called the colored funeral home, and the ambulance took her body there.

I looked around. Beth was standing in the doorway. Tears were pouring from her eyes. I still didn't believe Hebronetta was dead. She couldn't die. I know she had talked about the time to die, but those words of antiquity from the Book of Ecclesiastes didn't apply to Hebronetta Sikes. All I had to do was to go to the cabin. She would be sitting by the stove. A pot of beans would be simmering. Everything would be just like it always had been and always would be. She would be there to listen to me. To talk to me about Catie. To walk along the creek. To joke at me as we listened to the whispers of the corn.

I walked out the back door and went straight to Clear Creek. Just to show myself that everything was okay, I climbed the oak tree and hooted three times. Within seconds Kern and Tipps arrived, as I knew they would. Like always, the three of us sprinted up the creek to Hebronetta's little valley. When I got in sight of the cabin, I stopped. There was no smoke rising from the chimney. Slowly, the three of us walked toward Hebronetta's house. Within a few yards from the porch, the dogs lost their friskiness and began slinking forward, whining, their tails between their legs. They looked at the cabin then at me, trying their best to tell me what had happened.

The front door was unlocked, so I pushed it open and went in. I felt the chill of the room more than I had felt the cold outside. The absence of heat accented the empty feeling I got from looking around the cabin. On the table were scissors, several pages of the sports section, and some pictures which had already been clipped out. I sat down and looked at photos of New

Year's Day bowl games. For a long time I worked cutting out the remainder of the football pictures. When I finished, I walked around the room, carefully placing them on the already-covered walls. I then lay down on the bed and stared at the ceiling and the walls until I went to sleep sobbing.

When I woke up, it was pitch dark, and it took a few scary seconds before I realized where I was. I sat on the edge of the bed with pictures of Hebronetta flashing through my head and my chest beginning to ache from the loss. On the way outside, I hit my thigh on the corner of the table, and the pain was excruciating. Finally, I was able to reach the door and push it open. Outside was the darkest dark I had ever seen. A dense winter fog had set down in the valley and wiped out whatever light there might have been. I remembered that I had left my watch at home. I had no idea what time it was, but even if I had had my watch, I wouldn't have been able to see it. For awhile I stood at the edge of the porch trying not to panic while I decided what to do. I whistled and called and hooted for the dogs. No response. I put my hands up in front of my face. I couldn't see them. Something mean and evil had done this. Maybe something had come for Hebronetta. Maybe it was Hebronetta. I called her name, but the fog trapped my voice like a solid fence, keeping it from traveling more than a few feet.

Silence.

Step by step, I moved into the yard. I tried to remember where everything was, but nothing came to me. I headed in what I thought was the direction of the trail that led to the creek. I slid one foot ahead of the other to feel the ground so I wouldn't drop off in a ditch. I felt an indentation. Getting got down on my hands and knees, I worked around it. It was the trail. I got back on my feet and began inching along. Gradually, the walking became easier. Something beside me whimpered and my head jerked toward the noise. The whimper came again out of the blackness. My hair felt like it was standing straight up, and I jumped back. My back foot went over the edge and I fell, landing on the side of my foot. A terrible pain shot through my ankle. I could feel something wet where my face had hit some brush.

Leaning against the dirt bank, I tried to get myself together. I listened. There was no sound. Whatever I had heard must have been a small animal or a branch creaking. I thought about how many times I had been on this creek and how there was nothing to be afraid of out here. I tried to convince myself that my only problem was the fog. I felt my ankle. It was sore and probably sprained a little, but it was not as bad as I had thought at first. I pulled myself up and sat down on the trail to think. My head was now clear. The grogginess of the sleep and the terror of waking up in such a dark place had left me. I remembered that fog settles in low spots, and above it there is usually lots of clear sky. If I traveled by way of the creek, I would be in the dark all the way, so I decided the logical thing to do would be to get to higher ground. If I could sit in the chair by the fire, I could face the gap. Then I could walk in that direction and climb out of the mess I was in.

I hadn't gone far because it took me almost no time to return to the cabin area. Groping around, I eventually touched the chair and sat down, facing what I supposed was my way out. It was then a terrible thought struck me. Where was Catie? Why hadn't she been here to help me? The thoughts became worse. What if Hebronetta and Catie had some connection I didn't know about? What if Catie had left forever when Hebronetta died? The fear of losing Catie dwarfed any fear I had of physical harm.

I pushed that thought aside. After thinking about landmarks such as trees and shrubs, I memorized what I would pass if I went straight across the valley and up the side of the hill to the moon gap. As I worked my way toward the gap, I thought a lot more about Catie than about getting out of my predicament. I began to climb. Suddenly I looked up and saw stars through the fog. Seconds later I was looking at a magnificent, cloudless sky with uncountable stars hanging up there assuring me everything was all right. I turned around and looked behind me. The valley, in contrast to the heavens, was like a cauldron, seething with the smoke from boiling acids. I limped home.

We buried Hebronetta on the 4th day of February, 1956, next to her husband, Homer Winslow Sikes, Sr. Thirteen of us, not including Catie, were there. Mr. Isbell, Dad, Earnie Wayne, his dad, one of the grave diggers and I carried the casket down the old, abandoned road that began up on top near Mrs. Ingram's place and wound down toward the creek.

Mother, Mrs. Isbell, Beth, Mrs. Evans, Mrs. Ingram, the other grave digger, and Mrs. Jewel Price followed behind us. Jewel Price was a black lady (we called them "colored" in those days) who lived in town. She was a staunch member of the colored Baptist church, and probably the only member left who had not given up on Hebronetta. She had first visited Hebronetta back in the early forties, and from what Hebronetta had told me, she had continued to walk down the worn path to see her at least once a month during all those passing years.

I know Catie was at the funeral, because I had talked to her the night before down at the creek. I had been relieved to see her silhouette above me on the opposite bank, but I still asked her where she had been when I was about to get myself killed in all that fog. Of course, I got no answer, but I was sure she knew by the tone of my voice that I wasn't very appreciative of her not helping me. As I think back about Catie, I realize that as sweet as she was, she had a mischievous streak in her, and she wasn't always perfect. Hebronetta would have said that was proof Catie was not an angel.

The grave diggers had come to the site earlier that morning and dug the grave. We set the casket on the ground on the opposite side of the hole from the fresh dirt. There were enough chairs for all the women except Beth, so they were able to sit up near the gravesite. I backed off a ways and sat beneath an oak so I could lean back and get a good view of the cabin, the valley, the grave and the sky. I remember thinking what a nice day it was to be buried.

The sky was blue with wispy, white cirrus clouds stretched across it like a thin veil. February days in Texas can give you a false sense of spring coming, and this was one of those days. That morning, I had seen daffodils beginning to bloom at our house, but I knew that two days later it could be sleeting. Hebronetta must have picked the day.

Mr. Isbell stood at the head of the casket with a Bible in his hand and spoke the eulogy:

"Almost everyone Hebronetta Sikes knew is right around this grave today. Hebronetta gave each of us something, something we will always treasure. She gave us a gift of herself, a gift of her time. And she gave us a way of looking at the world, a way that will make our lives better. When we look at our short lives on earth and compare that time with eternal time, we realize we are only a passing mist in the morning. But when we are fortunate enough to know someone like Hebronetta, we know that even that mist that's gone in a split second has the opportunity to make the world a better place, even if it touches only a few other lives. We honor Hebronetta today, knowing that she's now back with her husband, Homer, and her son, Junior.

"Last night I looked through the Bible trying to find what would be appropriate to read today. I found what I was looking for in Psalms. It seems that the author of Psalms 104, whoever he was, had a kinship with Hebronetta. I know she would have liked this."

Mr. Isbell began to read, and I listened and looked around as his voice boomed out over the place where my friend had lived and died.

"Bless the Lord, O my soul. . . ."

I wondered where the dogs were. Who would feed them?

". . . who stretchest out the heavens like a cur-
tain. . . . who maketh the clouds his chariot: who walketh
upon the wings of the wind. . . ."

From where I was sitting, I could look northward
and follow the tops of trees that lined the dry stream bed.
I could see where it met Clear Creek. I thought that it
wouldn't be long before they began to break out in
green. Just like Hebronetta said.

". . . He sendeth the springs into the valleys which
run among the hills. . . ."

The moon gap really wasn't much of anything, I
thought. It probably wasn't fifty feet above where I was
sitting. It's funny that we always referred to it as a gap
when all it was was a little dip in the hill where a small
drainage flowed through.

". . . The high hills are a refuge for the wild goats. . ."

I watched a hawk swoop down and land at the top of
a cedar just fifteen or twenty yards away. I measured
distance in yards because of football lines. I wondered
how a girl would measure how far it was to the hawk.
The hawk was large. Because of where the others were
sitting, they were unable to see it perched there.

". . . O Lord, how manifold are thy works! In wisdom
hast thou made them all: the earth is full of thy riches."

That hawk had the most piercing eyes. It was like it
was looking right at me. I stared back. Our eyes locked.
Mr. Isbell's voice faded. The eyes. I stared. I looked
away.

". . . The glory of the Lord shall endure forever: the
Lord shall rejoice in his works . . ."

Mr. Isbell finished and bowed his head before raising it as Earnie's dad began "Amazing Grace." Mrs. Price joined him, then everyone sang. The voices of the little crowd began to rise toward the naked tree tops. I remember thinking that I could almost see the melody. It was like the heat shimmering above a car top on a hot summer day. I looked up at the hawk and the song. The hawk flew away toward Clear Creek. Imagining the old hymn was close behind, I followed it until it disappeared into the tall, bare winter trees.

Hebronetta had a will. It said:
"My name is Hebronetta Magdaline Sikes. I am of sound mind, and I make this, my last will and testament.

"I don't think I have any debts, but if I do I want Mr. Isbell to pay them off. I have already given him money for my funeral so that won't cost anything.

"I appoint Mr. Isbell as my Executor. If he cannot do it, I would like for his wife Kathleen to do it.

"I give all of my property as follows:

1. To my nephew, Bobby Sikes of Detroit, Michigan, I give $50.00.

2. To my niece, Claudia McDade Johnson of Memphis, Tennessee, I give $50.00.

3. I give $25.00 each to my good friends, Billy Griffin and Beth Griffin.

4. With the rest of my money I would like for Mr. Isbell to see that Kern and Tipps are taken care of and that a tombstone is placed over my grave and over my husband's grave. Anything that's left, I would like for Mr. Isbell to send to the village where my boy, Homer Winslow Sikes, Jr., is buried. It is to be used to help keep up his grave. However, if possible I would like for him to do with my boy what we talked about. Mr. Isbell knows what I am talking about.

5. I give my land back to the Isbells.
                    Signed this 10th day of October, 1955.
                    Hebronetta Magdaline Sikes

P.S. I want Billy to have all my football pictures."

173

Mrs. Isbell told me how the will was written. Since Hebronetta couldn't read, she told Mrs. Isbell what she wanted done. Mrs. Isbell wrote it down, then Hebronetta copied it in her own handwriting. It took her a long time, Mrs. Isbell said.

Our final basketball game was in the middle of February. It was at home against Central, and, as always, regardless of team records, the gymnasium would be filled. McKinney had beaten us 49–44 in the next-to-the-last game. That had been our last chance to win again. Central had beaten us badly twice, and no one thought we could ever beat them. Their record was 23 wins and 0 losses. Our record was 2 wins and 18 losses. Central also had beaten two of the top teams in Dallas, and only Greenville had played them a close game. I think Central won that game by more than 20 points.

Coach Chambers, however, would not admit that he thought Central would beat us again. He lived by sets of platitudes in which he honestly believed. And he believed that if he could convince us of the truth of those sayings, we would become a successful basketball team. Coach Chambers had several that I remember, and I should remember them, because he repeated them daily. I can still picture him. He was a tall man, probably an inch or two over six feet. He had black hair, on which he used enormous amounts of Wildroot Cream Oil. Lots of times we had to stop practice and change balls because Coach had run his hands through his hair, then touched the ball. I can still see Coach Chambers' thin face and long neck, which had a huge Adam's apple. Each time before he said something serious, he would clear his throat and swallow. We would watch the Adam's apple bob up and down. Then before he spoke, he would look around, making eye contact with every boy. Following this ritual, he would begin: "Men, just remember this. They put on their pants the same way you do." At that point, he would pause for emphasis then slowly and emphatically say, "One leg at a time."

We would respond, "Yeah, yeah, that's right."

Or, he would say, "Men, just remember this if you never remember anything else. The bigger they are, the harder they fall."

And we would say, "Yeah, that's right. That's right."

Or, he would say, "It's not the size of the dog in the fight. It's the size of the fight in the dog."

In response, we would flex our muscles and say, "You got it. That's right." That one made us feel real tough.

Sometimes Coach Chambers would give us ten or twelve of those sayings in a row. One that Coach used before every game was, "Basketball is a mental game. It's all in the head. If you think you can, you can. If you think you can't, you can't. Think about that for awhile, men."

"All right! Yeah! Let's go out there and get 'em!"

The Monday before the final game on Thursday, Coach made a visit to the dressing room, where he rarely entered because of its smell. That Monday he came in while we were dressing and asked us to sit down. He waited patiently for us to take a bench, then he silently and seriously looked at each of us. With a somberness that was unusual even for him, he said, "Men, we're going to have closed practices this week."

Riley Briggs, one of our guards, asked, "What's that, Coach?"

"That means we are going to lock the doors to the gym and not let anyone in today, tomorrow and Wednesday."

I looked at Gary. He returned the glance, raising his eyebrows and pursing his lips in a sarcastic "wow" look.

Gerald Bolivar, a second team guard who played ahead of me, asked, "How come?"

Coach Chambers once more looked at each of us, then answered, "Because we are going to change our offense, and we don't want anyone to find out. We're going to surprise Central, men."

I wondered why we were going to lock ourselves in. There hadn't been anyone at our practices for two months. A couple of the dads who previously came almost every afternoon had quit coming a long time ago. Even Bubba Neale, the manager, had stopped watching several weeks before. Instead, he would sneak off to the ball room and read comic books. The only time he appeared was for statistic taking.

After the coach's talk, we left the dressing room and ran out onto the floor for the Monday practice. As always, we first huddled around the coach at center court. He said, "Men, you've heard me say all year that if they don't have the ball, they can't score." A couple of the players said, "Yes, sir." Coach raised a fist and shook it. He squinted his eyes and stuck his lower lip out in a tough guy manner before saying, "Well, Thursday night, they aren't getting the ball."

"How come?" said Riley.

"Because we are going to stall. The whole game, if necessary," said Coach Chambers. With a stone face, he moved his head and looked each of us in the eye, one at a time.

In the game of basketball, a stall refers to a strategy where the team with the ball tries to keep it as long as it can. The players pass and dribble, but they don't shoot unless they have a shot that is so easy it can't be missed. On our team, that would mean we would never shoot. Most of the time, the stall is used at the end of the game when the team that is ahead keeps the ball so the other team can't score. In far fewer situations, the stall is used by an inferior team either to keep the score down or to possibly affect the superior team in such a way that the poorer team can win. Coach Chambers said we were trying to win, but I suspect that he really wanted to have a closer game.

I didn't care one way or another what happened. As I seldom got to play, it was unlikely I would play on Thursday night against Central. Mainly, though, I was just too much in love to care about basketball. My whole life was Catie. I thought of her while I was in class. I thought of her during practice. All the way home on the bus, I would look out the window and dream of her. I wanted to walk and hold hands with her. I wanted to sit beside her at the picture show. I wanted to dance with her. Most of all, I wanted to kiss her. I thought that if I could kiss Catie, I would never want anything else in my life. I never told her any of this. I did talk about movies and dances and dates, but I never mentioned kissing. I wondered a lot about what she thought, and whether she felt the same way about me, but I never asked her, and if I had, I wouldn't have received an answer.

The night before the game I had a dream. It was one of those strange dreams where everything seems so real, even though most things are out of place. In it, Hebronetta, Beth, Catie, Gary and I were sitting around a table in a classroom. The game with Central was just about to start, and I had to take a test before I could put on my uniform. I suddenly realized that I had not studied the entire six weeks, and I was beginning to panic. The game was only an hour away. Hebronetta was frantically trying to tutor me. Catie and Beth were looking for my basketball shoes. They were afraid I had left them at the house. The bell rang, and Gary walked out of the room. I started to get up and leave with him, but as I looked down I saw that I was naked. I froze. I tried to hide myself. Hebronetta continued to drill me in grammar. Through the window, I could see people going into the gymnasium. I couldn't move from my chair. Beth and Catie were laughing at me.

I woke up. My heart was beating like a machine gun. I lay there, relieved that it was only a dream. I thought of telling Hebronetta about it and laughed to myself, then felt a wave of depression when I remembered she was dead. A few seconds later, I jumped out of bed, dressed, went downstairs and slipped out the back door toward the creek. There was enough early morning light in the eastern sky for me to find my way over the hills and down to the creek. I walked fast toward Hebronetta's. When I reached the clearing below the cabin, I stopped. The cabin barely stood out in the fog-like gray of the dawn. Everything around me was so quiet and still. I called out for Kern and Tipps but was answered only with a weak echo of my own voice. The Isbells had been feeding the dogs, so I guessed they were off somewhere up there roaming around. I slowly approached the house, carefully observing everything within my sight. Quietly I said, "Hebronetta?" Then I listened for a response. There was none. Gradually I increased the volume until finally I shouted, "Hebronetta, where are you?" The only response was winter silence. There was not even a breeze to rustle some noise.

The sun was rising fast over the hills as I walked up on the porch and went inside. The walls were bare except for a few scraps of paper still hanging. Dust covered the table and chairs, and the droppings of mice were scattered on the floor. The room was cold and musty. When humans leave a house, it doesn't take long to lose all evidence of habitation. It might as well have been a house abandoned for a hundred years.

"Hebronetta, you've got to be around here. Give me some hint. Show me a shadow. Are you an animal? You can't just leave me like you did.

"We play Central tonight. I won't play probably, but I would have taken you if I could have. I'll take Catie. Why don't you come with her? We'll get clobbered, but you'll like the crowd. Everybody will be there.

"Hebronetta, please give me some kind of sign. I know you're down here when I walk around. I swear you were that hawk I saw at your funeral. Mr. Isbell did a nice job, didn't he? Mrs. Ingram said he did real well for an Episcopalian. She's kinda prejudiced. Thinks her church is the only way."

I got no response.

"Well, I'm leaving and going to school. I'll look for some sign."

All the way back home I listened and looked and smelled. If she had given me any indication of her whereabouts, I would have noticed it. I felt pretty empty by the time I got home. I had the feeling that Hebronetta was really gone.

The gym where my junior high team played was an old wooden structure that had, at one time, been the women's gym for the college. It had also been used for the men's games until a new one had been built in 1950. The backboards, like most in those days, were wooden. The stands were also wooden, but permanent. Beneath them were storage rooms. On one side of the court the seats had been removed, and this area was used for dances, ping pong, gymnastics and other things. During games, both teams sat on that side, opposite the crowd. When we played Central, temporary bleachers were brought in and placed on the side where the team benches were.

Almost every student wore our school color, blue, the day of the Central game, even though our chances of winning were near impossible. We knew that if we participated in activities, the day would be easy. There were pep rallies first period, noon and sixth period. During the other periods most teachers let us play games or watch movies, and we students were smart enough to go along with the school spirit thing. I suppose kids still do that today.

Bad news made the rounds early that morning. Walter Richter, one of our two starting forwards, was not at school. His mother had called and said he had a bad case of flu and would not be in school or at the game. Walter really wasn't a very good player, but we were counting on him to fight if that became necessary. A game with Central would not be normal if there wasn't a fight, and Walter was probably the only player other than Gary who could stand up to the Central players.

Earlier in the week I had told Catie about the game, and even though I said it was going to be a massacre, I asked her to go. I thought she would enjoy watching a game since she had been such a good player, and I knew she liked basketball because of what she had done to me in the driveway. I told her I was going with Mother, Dad and Beth and she would have to be there early, since we wanted to see the preliminary eighth grade game.

When we left for the gym that evening, I was down in the dumps. Catie wasn't with us. I always knew when she went somewhere with me because not only would I get a strong, inexplicable feeling of her presence, but sometimes I could even smell her perfume. I experienced neither that night. Even so, as my dad drove us to the gym, my spirits rose a bit. After some thought, I had decided it was probably okay that Catie was not going along. The game was going to be embarrassing, and if by some chance I got to play, it would be even more embarrassing. Central's second team was much better than our first team.

The entrance to the gym was just across the sidewalk from the street. You entered almost underneath the north basket. At the other end of the court were the coach's office and equipment room, the girls' locker room, and the boys' locker room. The latter was a large space surrounded on three sides by moveable metal lockers, and on the remaining side by showers, commodes and urinals. Long benches ran parallel to the lockers, forming a U in the room. The floor was concrete and had a drain in the center. It sloped from the showers and continued sloping past the drain toward the far wall.

If water didn't go into the drain, it headed west until it found a stopping place in front of the lockers. Usually it sat there until it evaporated. Sometimes, but not very often, a janitor would mop it up. The addition of standing water to a locker room of already dirty, damp shorts and socks and shirts and shoes used by junior high boys created a powerful stench that only a junior high boy could bear. We attributed the brevity of Coach Chamber's pre-game pep talks to the odor. The team always dressed during the fourth quarter of the first game and usually Coach just stuck his head in long enough to quote a couple of platitudes.

The night of the Central game was different. Coach Chambers, carrying a handkerchief in his hand, marched into the locker room in front of us. While we dressed, he pulled up three chairs and placed them where they faced the west wall. One of the chairs was for the coach. One was for Bubba Neale, the head manager. The other was for Charles Pruett, the assistant manager. At that time I thought of Charles as an obnoxious, little brown-noser who lived for the opportunity to report any infraction of the rules to the coach. Lots of times I griped about him to my parents. My dad would always respond to my judgmental attitude by quoting the father in *The Great Gatsby*: "Whenever you feel like criticizing any one, just remember all the people in this world haven't had the advantages you've had." I still didn't like Charles. Now, however, after all these years, I have fond memories of him. I discovered as I grew older that many of those persons who were different added some spice to my life and became the subject of enjoyable memories.

Even so, I'm not sure Charles Pruett would be a favorite of mine.

Charles had an objectionable habit of echoing the coach's words and making comments to him while Coach was talking to the team. Bubba was different from Charles in every way. Bubba was the player's man. He always cheated on statistics in order to help us out. If we had to make 18 out of 25 free throws to keep from running laps or doing push ups, Bubba's chart always listed us with at least 18 free throws. If we had to run 20 laps around the gym, Bubba always said, "finished" after no more than 13 or 14 had been completed. Coach Chambers never did the counting. When Charles tried to point out the miscalculations to Coach Chambers, Bubba would look at him and snarl, "You must be mistaken, Charles." Coach Chambers trusted Bubba completely.

Once, after Sherman had beaten us 62–46, Coach Chambers, trying to look on the bright side of a bad night, studied Bubba's shot chart. He congratulated us for making 26 of 49 shots from the field and 14 of 20 free throws. Charles kept saying there was a mistake. Coach Chambers said, "Charles, Bubba says you must be mistaken." As you have probably guessed, our coach did not teach math.

Coach Chambers stood silently facing us. After we were all seated, he cleared his throat, a signal to be quiet. Holding the handkerchief over his nose, he commenced his stare at the boys on the left end of the bench and, allotting at least five seconds to each player, he worked his way through the entire team. Charles sat there, never taking his eyes off the coach. Bubba looked up and rolled his eyes then looked down at a 12-pound shot that was between his feet. As soon as the coach's eyes left each player's eyes, most of us watched Bubba push the steel ball back and forth, from the inside of one foot to the other. Coach Chambers began, "Men, this game tonight will affect you the rest of your lives."

Charles said, "Yes, sir!"

Bubba rolled his eyes and spread his feet even more, giving the shot more distance to roll.

The coach continued, "What you do tonight, how you play in front of all these fans, will determine not only how people will think of you, but how you think of yourself. Just remember this if you never remember anything else. If you think you can, you can. If you think you can't, you can't."

Charles echoed, "If you think you can, you can. If you think you can't, you can't."

Bubba whispered to him, "Shut up." He almost lost control of the shot when he leaned toward Charles.

The coach continued, "Men, these Central boys put on their pants just like you do. One leg at a time. Think about it."

Charles said, "One leg at a time. Think about it."

Bubba leaned over and said rather loudly, "Quiet, dumb ass."

We all heard him and gasped in unison. Coach, who didn't tolerate anything off color, looked at Bubba and asked, "What did you say, Bubba?"

"I said, 'Some get what they ask.'"

"That's right, if you think you can, you can. If you ask, it's yours."

At that moment, Coach asked that we bow our heads for the pre-game prayer. As soon as he closed his eyes, Bubba gave us all a big wink, and we all gave him grins in return. Then we closed our eyes and listened to our coach begin subtly asking God for a victory. A few sentences into the prayer a new sound began to compete with his supplications. It was a small roar that sounded like a bowling ball traveling down the alley. Everyone looked up. Even the coach stopped praying and opened his eyes. Bubba had lost control of the shot, and it was rolling across the floor past the drain, picking up speed.

Riley, who was sitting next to me, was right-handed and a real good baseball player. He was also a clown. When the shot was half way past the drain, heading right toward him, he stood up and went into a shortstop crouch as he bent down to field the shot. At the last second before it reached him, he did a little dance and switched hands, picking the shot up with his right hand. Everyone had forgotten about the prayer and was laughing at Riley. That is until his face turned from a grin to a grotesque look of pain. He yelled as he pulled his hand up. The shot had split Riley's hand between the middle finger and the ring finger. Blood splattered everywhere. Bubba went running to the equipment room for a first aid kit, and Coach Chambers pressed a towel against the wound. The rest of us just huddled around looking first at Riley then at Coach to see his reactions. Bubba came back in with the first-aid kit and a doctor he had found in the stands. With only a glance at the hand, the doctor said, "Looks like you won't be playing tonight, son."

Coach Chambers reacted as if he had been the one cut up. The players stood there stunned. We heard Bubba say, "Oooh, shit!" under his breath.

When we ran out onto the floor for the pre-game warmup, the roar was unbelievable. I thought the noise couldn't get any louder, but then the Central team came out. The Central fans were yelling, stomping on the wood bleachers with their feet, blowing horns, and beating drums. If I had talked to myself, I wouldn't have been able to hear.

I knew they had a lot to yell about when I watched them do their lay-up drills. All of their players seemed to glide down the court. Their passes were perfect, and they didn't miss their shots. They shouted aloud the number of baskets they made in a row. They reached 25. I noticed one player I hadn't seen before. He was skinny and over six feet tall. I turned away when I saw him dribble behind his back and lay-up the ball with his left hand. My eyes caught Bubba's. He wiped his forehead with the back of his hand then looked up and placed his hands in a prayer position. I knew he had seen the new player.

Before the game, both teams lined up at the double water fountain. There was a lot of laughing and joking, because most of the players on both teams knew one another. Except for the new guy, I knew them all by name but I had never talked with any of them, so I just stood and watched in awe. It seemed as if every one of the Central players shaved. I had just started a couple

189

months before and only on my upper lip. Our cheerleaders, who were standing nearby, stared at the Central players as if they didn't even know we existed.

In those days, some of the rules were different. There was no three-point shot. After each tie ball and at the beginning of each half and each quarter, there was a jump ball. In the backcourt, the referee didn't have to touch the ball before it was thrown in bounds. Other than that, the game was just about like it is today.

Taking Riley's place in the starting line up was Jack Owens, a kid about my size who was said to have been an excellent player back in elementary school. Unfortunately, he had never grown another inch since sixth grade. Dwain Richey was the first-team center. As well as I can remember, he was about 5'11" and a pretty good player, except for an inability to use his left hand. Walter Richter's sub was Randy Joe Dotson, who was slow and fat and very unaggressive. As Bubba said, "We went from a D player to an F player when Walter got sick." The other starter, besides Gary, was Joe Pat Thompson. Joe Pat really stood out in warmup drills. He looked mature, fast, and skilled and confident. Those apparent qualities quickly disappeared when the game started. Joe Pat could do almost nothing when he was guarded. I suppose his looking good in warmups was enough for Coach Chambers to overlook his game skills.

The game began ominously with Central getting the tip and scoring before three seconds had gone from the clock. After their basket Gary brought the ball up court for us and stopped moving forward after he crossed the center line. He just stood there, dribbling. The stall had begun.

When a team stalls, the game becomes very boring. I can remember this one made me feel like sleeping and from where I was sitting on the far end of the bench I wouldn't have been noticed if I had dozed awhile. The stall did have some benefits, though. Central had not expected us to hold the ball, so they had some trouble adjusting to what we were doing. They weren't able to steal the ball, but they didn't need to take it away. If they waited long enough, usually not more than 30 seconds, we would throw the ball away or double dribble or take too many steps. The first quarter ended with us behind 12–5.

During the second quarter, I spent most of the time picking out people I knew in the stands. I also tried counting the number of people sitting there, but they kept moving around too much. Almost everyone was getting up and going to get popcorn and drinks. A few fans began to boo during the last minute of the second quarter.

We went to the locker room at half, trailing by only 12 points, 25–13. Coach Chambers followed us. He had a cocky smirk on his face when he told us we were doing great and asked us to sit down. We sat. He then went through his ritual of looking at each of us individually awhile. His Adam's apple bobbed up and down rapidly, as if it were trying to push out profound words that we knew were soon to come out of the his mouth. It finally stopped bobbing, and he spoke. "Men, I have a few things I want to say to you, and I want you to listen carefully." I thought he was getting ready to tell us how to beat Central. For the first time that night, I began to get excited. He went on, "And I want you to think about what I say before you go out on that floor the second half." He became much louder than usual: "I want you to win this game." All of us were hanging on his words.

He continued very slowly. "Listen men. First, there is no failure except in no longer trying. Secondly, I'm a great believer in luck. The harder you work, the more you have." He waited for a response from his players, but there was none since most of us were trying to figure out what he meant. "Third, the big shots are only the little shots who keep shooting. Chew on that one awhile men."

Gary said to me under his breath, "Then why are we stalling?" I shrugged my shoulders, and raised my eyebrows in a question. Then I went back to being bored.

"And fourth, when the game gets tough, the tough get going."

With that, Coach stopped and looked at us silently, tightening his jaw in a way that let us know that he knew he had imparted the secret of success to his pupils. He left after telling us to think quietly for a minute or so on what he had just said.

Bubba thought the Coach had gotten pretty deep with that talk. Gary was more interested in who the new kid was, since he had scored more than half of Central's points. Charles told us that his sources indicated the new player was a transfer from Hobson's Prairie, which was a little town a few miles outside Oakpoint. Charles said the new kid was also sixteen years old. While this conversation was taking place, Gary walked to the door and ran back to tell us that Central and the referees were on the floor waiting for the jump ball.

We heard only a few scattered cheers from the crowd as we ran out onto the floor. They had obviously and probably wisely given up on us. After the tipoff we settled back into our stall, and I settled down on my end of the bench to watch the last half. Our team played pretty well, but midway in the third quarter, Dwain fouled out. Only seconds before the quarter ended, Randy Joe waddled to the bench with his fifth foul. When the fourth quarter began, the score was 37–20. By that time I had resigned myself to the fact that I was not going to play, and I started thinking of Catie. I was really glad she was not there. Beth was, though, and she hadn't given up on me yet. She had moved over to the temporary stands behind our bench and was shouting, "We want Billy. We want Billy." I kept turning around and motioning for her to be quiet.

I had just signaled my disapproval to her for the third time, when I turned around and saw one of the strangest things I had ever seen. Coach Chambers had told us at the end of the quarter to get out of the stall, start running and start scoring. We were only 17 points behind. Joe Pat had taken a pass and was dribbling fast down the side in front of our bench when he just seemed to explode. His middle went back like he had been hit in the stomach. The air went out of him with a wooof sound, then he doubled up and fell to the floor gasping for air. The ball flew out of bounds, but no one paid any attention to it. They were looking at Joe Pat, who was on his back, writhing around, struggling to catch a breath. Coach Chambers, the doctor, and Joe Pat's parents ran to him. As the doctor checked him, he started breathing again. The doctor said it looked like he had the breath knocked out of him, but just to be on the safe side, he suggested that Joe Pat should go out of the game.

There was no one left to go in at that position but Billy Griffin. Even so, Coach Chambers looked up and down the bench several times. Finally, after putting his hand over his mouth and musing, he said, "Billy, come here."

What happened next probably still causes a few Oakpoint people to shake their heads in bewilderment, even to this day thirty-six years later. Only I can explain what really happened, and this is the first time I have ever done so.

Those who have spent their athletic careers as substitutes will understand the mixed feelings that you have when you are called. You want very much to play, and you've always dreamed of being a star, but deep down inside, you know that the dream is not realistic. You never quite admit it, though. Then, when you are called, the reality of what you really are comes rushing up through you, mixing with the dreams and usually pushing them aside.

That's what happened to me the night of the Central game. I was comfortable being a spectator. It was not a threatening role. When Coach Chambers called my name, fear took me over. I went from wanting to be a hero to wanting not to be a goat. The world stopped as I walked toward the Coach. He placed his arm around me, leaned over next to me, and said, "Billy, we can still win this game. I want you to forget what your opinions of your skills are. I want you to remember that you are in better condition than any player we have. You are going to switch men with Gary. I want you to guard the new kid. Dog him all over the court. Try to keep him from getting the ball. Never let him get behind you. If he gets the ball, stick with him and try to make him pick up his dribble."

"Yes, sir," I gulped.

"And Billy, remember this. If you think you can do it, you can. Now get in there."

He swatted me on the butt as I started toward the scorer's table.

I looked up at the score board. It read 39–22. Seven minutes and thirty-two seconds remained in the game. Central had the ball out of bounds in the backcourt. I got up close to the new kid. The referee handed the ball to the boy who was throwing it in, blew the whistle, and the game resumed. The new kid walked right into me then popped back toward our basket so quickly that he put ten feet between us in less than half a second. He easily received the pass and started his dribble up court. I was in the proper defensive position, watching his stomach, not his head, just as I was supposed to do. He put the ball right to the floor and started to his right, then before I had a chance to react, he was going to his left, leaving me behind. I started to run to catch up, and there, right in front of me was the ball, with the new kid ten feet in front of it trying to stop and come back. I grabbed it and turned, heading full speed for the basket. My lay-up went in perfectly. 39–24.

A Central boy jumped out of bounds, grabbed the ball and turned to throw it up court. I had already messed up. My player was at half court, and I was not even close to him. When I saw the boy release the ball, I turned and ran toward the new kid, who had his hands up ready to catch it. But it didn't get to him. It dropped right in front of me. I took it and turned toward the basket. Gary was all alone, and I threw him the ball. He laid it in with no opposition. 39–26. The noise was getting a little louder. The new kid stepped out of bounds and threw the ball in. He faked me perfectly, but the ball seemed to hit some invisible wall and bounce right into my hands. I took one dribble and scored. The crowd was not moving around anymore. Fans abandoned the concession stand. Central called time out. Only six minutes were left.

The next five and a half minutes were unbelievable. Central lost the ball almost every time they got it. If they tried to dribble, the ball didn't go with them. It went bouncing away in a different direction, usually toward me. When they tried to pass, the ball would drop in mid-flight or change directions. Twice Central called time out. Their coach went out and examined the ball. He bounced it several times, then asked for a new one. Our last time out was called with 36 seconds to go. The score was 41–38. Central had the ball out. I stood in the huddle not listening to a word Coach Chambers was saying. I was grinning and looking around, looking for Catie. She had found her way to the gym.

The new kid got the ball and drove toward the basket. He went up over Gary and put the ball softly on the backboard. But it didn't go in. It bounced right off thin air on top of the basket and shot in a line drive toward half court. I picked it up and raced down to score. We were one point behind. Twenty seconds to go.

There is a different kind of noise on a basketball court than in the stands. The difference is not just a matter of degree but of species. In a small jam-packed gym, it comes from above, below, from all directions. When I made the shot that put us one point behind, the noise came in waves. I didn't just hear it. I felt it. It picked me up and carried me across the floor. It made me feel I could do anything. It gave me a memory that I will carry with me the rest of my life.

Central called their last time out with nine seconds left on the clock. There was little that Coach Chambers could do in the huddle. We couldn't hear a word he was saying. He was pointing at the floor, slapping us on the back, and yelling, but it was all in vain. Whatever he had in mind would never be used. If Central got the ball in, the game was lost.

The horn sounded. We walked to our positions. One guy was guarding the player who was throwing the ball in. Gary was covering the boy closest to the side line. I was on the opposite side with the new kid. The referee handed the ball to the Central player and raised his hand. He would lower it when the ball touched a player on the court. When his hand went down, the clock would begin running. The crowd became silent. Everyone was standing. I saw my mother with her hands over her face and my dad with his fingers locked together and his hands behind his head, his elbows sticking out in front like horns.

They got the ball in. Gary had slipped and let his man get away. He rushed toward him. I ran to help make a desperation foul. The Central guard looked to his right and saw the new kid wide open where I had left him. He threw a hard pass toward him. I couldn't get it.

But it dropped halfway and bounced toward mid-court. I lunged for it and grabbed it just as I peripherally saw the clock show two seconds. At mid-court, I bent my knees deeply and with two hands on the ball came up with all the strength I had. I let the ball go toward the basket.

A long shot in basketball is like a dream in a short nap. So many thoughts are compacted into a fleeting moment. The shooter has lots of things to think about while the ball is in the air. As the ball left my hands, my heart jumped right through my head. I had that special feeling that told me the shot was going in. But I soon saw I was wrong. My heart dropped. The ball was traveling a bit to the right, and it was going to be short.

My whole being sunk as I heard the game-ending buzzer. Then something strange happened, and only I, from my position on the floor, could see it. The ball almost imperceptibly slowed down. It moved slightly to the left and changed its downward angle, moving up slightly. Like it was being carried. It stopped spinning and traveled straight to the basket. The ball went through softly and perfectly, not touching any of the rim and barely ruffling the net.

The place exploded. First, the noise knocked me over, then the fans did. I looked around. The Central players were standing in disbelief. Their coach had his hands on his head, looking at the basket like he had been hypnotized. Within seconds I was lifted off my feet and carried around the court by Wanton and Mr. Norton. All the other players and Coach Chambers were being carried around and around the gym. Charles had been hoisted up to the south basket, and he was cutting the net. After each cut, he would turn around and throw both hands high into the air. It was the most exciting moment in my life, and thanks to Catie, whom they never knew, one of the most exciting times most of my friends would ever experience.

Our 1956 annual, "Tiger Stripes," has a full page picture of the celebration that followed the Central game. Charles is cutting the net. Coach Chambers is hugging the cheerleaders. Gary is on someone's shoulders. Bubba told me he thinks the left arm that sticks out into the picture on the left side of the page is mine.

One day in late February, the wild plums appeared in the creek bottom, their white blossoms signaling a change. The bright green winter wheat on the far side of the valley added another color. Then in early March, the redbuds came out. I could smell a newness in the earth as it readied itself to burst out in green. All kinds of changes were coming. And going. I had had my season of being a hero, and that part of my life was fading fast.

March went quickly by. Dad and Mother wanted a garden, and I helped them plow some land northeast of the house. I spent many hours along the creek, fishing for crappie when they made their run upstream from the lake. I also spent many hours doing nothing but wandering around looking at clouds and budding trees and water and thinking about Catie. Sometimes Beth would go with me. Sometimes I would meet Earnie, and we would roam. Once, he and I went to the forks several miles below our place where Clear Creek met another stream. Almost every night I met Catie down by the rock. It was by then perfectly natural talking with her, but I was beginning to have some vague feelings of hopelessness. Each time these feelings surfaced, I would look at her pictures, and they would pull me out of the depths. Even so, my moods were like a roller coaster.

In early April we received our school pictures, and on one of them I wrote "To Catie—Love, Billy 1956." I took it to the tree in the meadow and placed it in the hole. Beside it I put a Dixie cup filled with water and pansies from Mother's garden. I also left a note telling

Catie I was going to the creek Saturday morning and asking her to meet me at the tree.

That night I slept restlessly. The moon was full, and since I had left my windows open, the room was covered with soft white light. I was awakened some time after midnight by a night bird, I suppose a mockingbird. It sang for what seemed like forever, and I couldn't get back to sleep. I lay there watching the sky and listening to the night sounds. My door was open, and the breeze from the south came into my room and left from my windows, pressing the drapes against the screen as it headed north. I watched them drop, then try to blow outward as another gust came and pushed them. While I lay there, I thought about a lot of things. I wondered why all this had happened to me. I wondered if other Caties came to see other boys in the world. I wondered how many other boys were in love with ghosts. I thought about what it must be like for Catie. If she felt the same way toward me as I felt toward her, then her sadness must be even greater than mine. At least I wasn't completely alone as she was. I drifted off to sleep thinking about walking the hills holding hands with Catie.

I dreamed about her all night, even when I returned to sleep after the whistle of the five A.M. train, far off to the east. By the time I left the house the next morning, the sun was already high in the eastern sky. I watched it disappear and reappear as it slipped in and out of the fast-moving low clouds blowing in from the south. It was a cool morning, and the perfume of spring was everywhere.

The picture and the flowers were gone. I smiled when I saw the empty spot, and Catie must have seen me smiling, because immediately I knew she was there. It was almost as if I could hear the wind blowing her skirt, as if I could reach out and touch her. I told her it would be a nice day to go to the creek, and when we left the tree and walked up toward the highest point, I remember saying, "Wouldn't it be nice to be able to bottle a morning like this and keep it for hot August days or bad days in winter?"

I continued making small talk, knowing that Catie was listening. "Last night a bird sang for hours outside my window. Did you hear it?"

We reached the top of the ridge above the creek bottom where the trees were getting their first green. I stood there and looked east toward the forks, then west in the direction of Hebronetta's. There was still enough morning haze to give the illusion of one hill after another.

"Catie, I love this place," I said, as if I was talking to the whole world.

"So do I. Especially on a spring morning."

I felt icy rain drops touching my arms, but there weren't any rain clouds, and my arms weren't wet. It felt kind of like wind chimes would if you could feel them instead of hearing them.

I was almost afraid to turn around. When I did, not more than ten feet from me was Catie Waldrop. I couldn't say a word. I could only stare. Catie was as surprised as I. She looked down at herself and felt her dress. She ran her left hand up her right arm, then her

right hand up her left arm. She grinned then placed her
hands over her mouth to control her excitement. She
then ran them through her hair.

I said, "You really *are*, Catie."

"I guess I am. I really am, Billy," she said, happiness
just bursting out all over her. Both of us alternated
looking at the ground then quickly looking at each other.
She was as shy as I was.

I finally was able to speak some more. "Your hair is
redder than I thought," I told her. She didn't respond.
"An' you've got more freckles." Catie appeared a little
hurt. I quickly said, "I like freckles and red hair." She
wrinkled her nose at me and grinned.

"Where are we going?" Catie asked.

"I guess we'll keep going to the creek. That all
right?"

"Sure."

We walked a while in silence. I kept my hands stuck
in my front pockets, and every once in a while I would
steal a glance at Catie, and sometimes we stole glances
at each other at the same time and exchanged embarrassed smiles when our eyes met. It was sure harder to
talk with a real girl than with a ghost.

"I had forgotten how good the wind feels," Catie
said, turning around to face the south, lifting her head
and putting her arms out, her eyes closed.

"Yeah, it does," I agreed, mad at myself that I
couldn't respond any better.

She turned back toward the north. "I used to fish
right down there in that hole of water," she said, pointing to the stream below us.

"Yeah, Mr. and Mrs. Isbell told me."

"They're such nice people. I loved her almost as much as my mother."

"That's where I learned you were such a good basketball player."

Catie giggled, then said, "It's easy to be good when you're invisible. That was fun, but I kinda felt bad for those Central boys. They were really a lot better than your team."

"I know."

"You didn't get mad about my doing that, did you?" she said, looking at me.

I responded, finally able to make some eye contact. "No, not really. Not many people have something like that ever happen to them. My dad told me it was great but not to expect it to occur again. He said he'd never seen a team fall apart like Central did. An' he'd never seen such lucky bounces of the ball. Wonder what he'd have thought if I told him what really happened?"

"He wouldn't believe you. I still don't believe this myself, Billy."

"You don't either? Neither do I."

"Do you think maybe it happens to everybody?" Catie asked.

"I dunno, but if it does, I'd think someone would say something about it. How could anyone keep something like this secret?"

"Have you told anyone?"

"No, except for Hebronetta."

"So maybe everyone else doesn't tell either."

We crossed the creek, stepping on some flat rocks at the lower end of a pool. On the other side, we sat down on a bar of white sand. I lay back. Catie sat up, her knees folded in front of her, and flipped sticks and pieces of gravel into the water.

She talked, glancing at me every so often. "I used to sit along here for hours and feel the sun on my face. I remember it was so nice and warm, just like today. Sometimes I would go to sleep and wake up not knowing where I was." She was silent for a moment, then she asked, "Is this really 1956?"

"Yeah, April, 1956."

"Did you know that in 1938 there used to be beaver dams down here, and farther upstream, people used to trap mink, like they make coats out of?"

"Mr. Isbell told me something about that."

"I can remember seeing the dams, right down there nearer the bridge. . . . What's your favorite color, Billy?" Catie asked, changing the subject.

"I dunno. Green, I guess."

"Why?"

"I don't know. Just is."

"Mine's pink."

"How come?"

"One time Mama bought me a pink dress. It was spring, just before we moved from here. I tried it on and even went over to Mrs. Isbell's and showed her. She said it was the prettiest dress she'd ever seen, and that every boy in town would chase me. She liked to tease. . . . I never got to wear it, though, since we moved away. It was so pretty."

I could tell that Catie was really thinking hard about that dress, but I was unable to respond to her feelings. Instead, I said, "Did you move after school was out?"

"Yes," she answered, still, I supposed, thinking about the pink dress she never wore anywhere.

"You know that day I went to sleep on that bar upstream, you know when I woke up an' saw you? How'd that happen?"

"I don't know. I was just spying on you and when you woke up, I could tell you saw me because you looked surprised and said something."

"Why'd you run?"

"I don't know. I guess I was scared."

"Why'd you always stay invisible?"

She didn't answer. She looked at me seriously and brushed a bug off my forehead. I just about melted into the sand when she did that. She said, "There're all kinds of bugs and stuff like that down here. I don't know why you couldn't see me. I don't know why you saw me that day at the creek, and I don't know why what happened today happened. I don't even know why I'm here."

"I'm glad you are," I said, surprised at my sudden boldness.

"Me, too," Catie said as she picked up some sand and let it run out of her hand like sand in an hour glass. "Have you ever thought about how good sand feels?"

"I like to lie on the sand and stick my feet in the water. It's kinda like being at the beach," I said.

"Did you ever go to the beach?"

"Uh huh. We went to Galveston twice when we lived in Dallas. I got sunburned, but it was fun."

207

"I bet it was. I read about it, but we never went. My dad gave me a shell one time, though. He said if you put it to your ear, you could hear the sound of the surf. I used to do that a lot."

"It does sound like the sea. I used to do that, too. Beth still does."

I asked Catie if she wanted to walk some more, and she said yes, so we started upstream on the north side of the creek. I was close to her, but I avoided touching her even though I really wanted to hold her hand. It wasn't as easy as I imagined it would be. All I had to do was just reach out and grab her hand, but I couldn't do it. I was wondering so much what she was thinking about and whether what I would say would be the right thing, that I didn't even talk.

Only a short way up the creek was a small drainage, nothing more than a gulley, that came in from the north. It was too wide to jump, and in order to cross it, you had to go into it and then climb up the steep opposite side. I went first and turned to help Catie. She gave me her hand, and I pulled her up. And when she reached the top, she didn't let go. She moved her hand and locked her fingers tightly with mine. I'm sure I turned a bright red, but I said nothing, and neither did Catie. I was hoping and praying it would take us a year to get across that field.

After a while, we went back across the creek and up the side creek to Hebronetta's. As we stood looking down at Hebronetta's grave, I said to Catie, "Hebronetta

helped me find out about you. She and I sat down there,"
I said pointing to the circle of rocks where she had built
fires, "and looked at the moon at the right time, then at
the stars at the right time. She told me how to communicate with you. How did she do that?"

"It was easy."

"Whadda ya mean?"

Catie was real close. She was facing me, still holding
my hand, looking straight at me since we were about the
same height. She giggled and wrinkled her nose again.
I thought she was the prettiest girl that had ever lived.
She said, "Do you remember those three chairs over
there by the fire?"

"Uh huh."

"You were sitting on this side of the fire. Hebronetta
was on the other side."

"Yeah, I remember."

"Well, I was sitting next to her in the other chair,
listening to everything she said. You both were so
intense, looking at that moon. And she had such a nice
little rhyme about the ghost." Catie smiled at me. It was
a mixture of sweetness and mischievousness.

I said, "You mean you came to the tree because you
heard Hebronetta give the instructions?"

"Uh huh."

"And you heard her tell me to write you?"

"Uh huh."

"And you, on purpose, didn't answer me the first
time?"

"Uh huh."

"And you listened to Hebronetta tell me that I had to write in such a way that you could give me a yes or no answer?"

"Uh huh."

"So you were just having fun with me?"

"Uh huh."

"Catie, can I kiss you?"

"Uh huh."

She closed her eyes. I did, too.

I'm sure there was a lot of awkwardness about my first kiss, but I don't remember it because kissing her obliterated any thoughts I might have had about whether I was doing it correctly. I was kissing Catie, and that was all that mattered.

She moved her head back from me, looked me in the eye and said, "I never kissed a boy before."

"Me neither. I mean I never kissed a girl before."

"Let's do it again," she said. And we did.

Huge thunderheads had built up over us, but I didn't notice them. Nor did I notice the first raindrops, but Catie did and we ran to the cabin. We reached the porch just as a downpour began. Turning around, we watched the rain and talked.

"Catie, why can't you write anything but 'yes' and 'no'?"

"I can."

"But you didn't."

"I know," she said, placing her head on my shoulder then taking it away. "I didn't know whether to be bold or what. What if I had written you notes, and you didn't like me? I would have felt stupid."

"Like I felt when I wrote you that note or gave you those presents."

"I liked that." She paused and laughed a little laugh. "Didn't you figure that someone who could make books cascade off the shelf could write? You should have seen your face when those books started falling. I couldn't stop laughing all the way home."

I laughed.

After a while we went inside, where, because of the cloudy weather, the cabin was darker than usual. I sat down in one of the chairs. Catie sat down on the other side of the old wooden table. She said she was hungry, and I said I was, too. I told her I would go to the house and get some food. She could go with me, or I could bring it back. She said she wouldn't feel right going up there, and she was afraid of what might happen if I left her. She was scared she might not be there when I got back.

We looked around the pantry and found some pork and beans, spoons, old bowls, and a can opener. I had never had a better meal than I had on that rainy Saturday afternoon. When Catie finished, she pushed her bowl away and said to me, "My dad always said to me that days like this were good for stories. Do your parents tell you stories?"

"Yes," I said. "At least they used to. They've told me stories ever since I can remember. What kind of stories did you hear?"

"All kinds, but mainly ghost stories. They always scared me."

211

"I heard a lot of them, too."

"Do you want me to tell you one?" Catie asked.

"Sure," I said.

Catie was a serious storyteller and a good one. She told me about the lady in blue who appeared among the Indians of West Texas before the priests had ever visited them. When the first missionary priests arrived, the Indians already knew about Christianity. They said a lady in blue had come to them and taught them. One of the priests went back to Spain and, in a convent there, found a nun who would go into trances. She said that while in a trance she would be transported to the New World. She could even describe the Indians and name them. It was a strange story. Then Catie told me about an evil blanket that killed people by suffocating them. That one was pretty good, too.

"Billy, why don't you tell me one, a real scary one."

I thought a few seconds. "Okay," I said. "But you have to listen carefully."

"I will."

Still only halfway believing what was happening, I looked at Catie Waldrop across the table from me, then began. "Well, this took place in Austin. Austin has some big hills that start at the west side of town."

"I know. We went there once. Saw the Capitol, too."

"Anyway, there're some roads that go up on those hills, and a lot of the kids go parking up there."

"What's that?"

"You know, where they have dates and drive out at night and park their cars and listen to the radio and kiss. You know."

"Okay."

"Well, anyway, this boy and this girl are out parked, and they can look out over the city and see the lights, and it's real pretty, and they're listening to the radio. All of a sudden, the announcer interrupts. He has a special bulletin. A crazy, dangerous man has escaped from the insane asylum. He has killed a lot of people before, and he could do it again. Anyway, the announcer says the man was last seen heading for the hills. He warns everyone to get inside their houses and lock their doors. He says you can tell who the man is because he has had his right hand amputated, and he has a hook on it."

Catie was hanging on every word.

"The girl, she wanted to go home, but the boy, he thought he was brave, so he said no. It wasn't long, though, before the announcer came on again and said they knew the man was somewhere in the hills. Well, the girl got really scared. The boy didn't want to go, but she started crying. He got mad and started the car and burned out and left."

"What's 'burned out'?"

"That's where you push down on the gas pedal real hard and the wheels spin and the car shoots off real fast."

"Oh."

"He's mad, so he drives fast, right to her house. She's sitting beside him, so she gets out on his side."

"Why's he mad?"

"'Cause he wanted to stay and kiss."

"I don't blame him."

"But Catie, there's this crazy guy that could kill them."

213

"Yes, I guess so."

"Anyway, he drives home and gets out and goes inside and goes to bed. The next morning he gets up and goes out to wash his car, and there on the door handle of the passenger side is a hook. Then he hears on the radio that the crazy man was arrested and that he was in horrible pain because the hook was torn off him."

Catie just sat there. "You mean he was trying to get in?"

"That's it. See, when the boy burned out, the man was opening the door with the hook, and it tore it off him. If they had stayed a second longer, he would have got in the car and killed them."

"Oh, my Gosh!" Catie said, her eyes getting bigger. "That's scary." She jumped up and ran around the table and told me to scoot over so we could sit in the same chair. Just then a loud clap of thunder made the cabin shudder. We both jumped and Catie scooted up closer to me.

It wasn't uncomfortable at all sitting in the same chair with Catie, and it didn't seem to bother her either. We both put one of our elbows on the table and faced each other. Catie said, "Let me tell you one more story. This one's not scary. My mother told it to me when I was little."

She could have talked to me for the rest of time. All I wanted to do was sit there and look at her. I didn't care what she told me.

She began, "'Once upon a time' .... That's how Mama always started a story. Once upon a time there was a little lake. I think it was supposed to be in

Arkansas. It was very blue and very clear, and it was surrounded by beautiful green mountains that were reflected in the water. Around this lake lived all kinds of animals. There were 'possums and skunks and moles and squirrels, everything. There were spiders of all kinds and frogs and snakes. In the air were eagles and hawks and crows, and, of course, there were lots of fish in the water. There were no people around the lake at that time.

"Every night when there was no moon, the stars were so bright that if you looked into the water, you would have sworn that the stars were there instead of in the sky. On those dark nights, all the animals and birds and other things would surround the lake and just sit or stand for a long time looking at the stars in the heavens and in the water.

"There was one star that was the favorite of all the creatures. It was bright, and it always seemed to be overhead in the Milky Way when the night was darkest. And beside the big star was a little star that always followed it.

"Well, one night, all the creatures were gathered there. I'm gonna say 'creatures,' 'cause it takes too long to name everybody that was there. Is that okay?"

"Sure," I said. I hadn't taken my eyes off Catie.

"Let's see, did I say the creatures were by the lake?"

"Yeah."

"Okay, they were all watching when, all of a sudden, the little star fell out of the sky. They saw it as it shot across right by the rest of the stars. It got bigger and bigger, and it fell right into the middle of the lake. There it was, glowing down there. All the creatures from miles around came to see it. They came every night. One day, I mean night, the raccoon said that he had been looking up in the sky, and he could have sworn that the big star was crying. He told a frog and the frog told a deer and pretty soon everyone knew it. It's kinda like gossip. Anyway, all the animals looked up, and sure enough they, too, thought the big star was crying. They had a lot of meetings and talked about it and decided that the reason it was crying was that its baby had fallen from the sky. Do you follow this okay?"

"Yes, Catie." She had the bluest eyes.

"Good. You know what the creatures decided to do? They decided to try to get the little star back into the sky. But it was a tough job. You can just imagine how difficult that would be. They had to think hard and do a lot of planning. After much trial and error they succeeded. Can you guess how?"

"I have no idea."

"Well, all the spiders spun giant webs, and the fish carried the web to the bottom and somehow got it under the little star. Then all the fish grabbed some of the web, and they pulled the star to the surface, where the frogs took over. You know how frogs do? They blow up this little sac on their chin. Have you seen that?"

"Uh huh, lots of times."

"So the frogs were like inner tubes, and they held the star at the top. The forest animals had lines that they held so the little star wouldn't sink. Then all the birds came down and grabbed ahold. They lifted that little star right out of the water and up into the sky. Way high up, the eagles and hawks and even the buzzards took over. They flew so high that they met some stars floating by. They talked to the stars, and told the stars where the little one belonged. The stars then took over and carried the little star back to his mama.

"Now, if you're at this little lake on dark nights, you can look up and see the big star and the little star. And just about midnight, if you look closely, you can see the big star flash a little brighter a few times. That's her way of saying thank you. Mama said you can even see it over Texas. She said that when you see the star brighten, it means everything is all right. And that's the end of the story. Did you like it, Billy?"

"It was good, Catie. I really liked it."

"My grandmother told it to my mama and told her to tell it to her daughter, and my mama told me to tell. . . ." Catie stopped and looked down. I couldn't think of anything to say, so I just reached over and squeezed her shoulder.

The storm passed, and we went outside where I sat on the edge of the porch. Catie walked into the little meadow and picked wildflowers. The sky was clearing in the west. It was purple toward the east, an indication that it was still raining hard in that direction. A cool front would probably blow in later in the day.

The rain had cleared the air and brought out all the smells of spring. I watched Catie. She was whistling. Sometimes she would look up and wave to me. She came back smiling and gave me a handful of Indian paint-brushes and daisy-like fleabane. I didn't know their names then, but I learned them later and never forgot.

217

"Billy, you ever have warts?" she asked.

"Warts?" Catie came up with the darndest change of subjects.

"Yes, those things that grow on your fingers?"

"That's what I thought you said. I had some a couple years ago. Got 'em taken off," I said, looking at my left hand to see if there was any scar left. "Why'd you ask that?"

"I was just thinking. There was a lady that lived on the other side of the creek. My Mama would take me up there, and the lady would take off the warts."

"You mean she would cut them off?"

"No, that's why I'm telling you this. She would give me a pin for each wart and say, 'Now the wart's mine.' In a couple weeks they'd be gone."

"I've heard of stuff like that, but I never believed it really happened. Just stories."

"Well, it did. I promise."

"I guess it could happen," I said, thinking a few seconds before I spoke. "You know, come to think of it, Mr. Isbell told me about this guy who lives around here that can stop bleeding. He says if an animal or person is bleeding, the man can look at the wounds then take a string and turn around and tie the string a certain way. He says some magic words, and the bleeding stops."

"Do you believe that?"

"I don't know. Mr. Isbell told me."

"Well, I believe things like that can happen, Billy. . . . You wanna go over to that lady's house I was talking about?"

We left Hebronetta's meadow without looking back. I was too absorbed in Catie. When we reached the creek, it had risen some, so we had to take off our shoes and wade across. We held hands and continued talking as we crossed the big field. Usually I was conscious of things around me. I can always remember what a day was like, how the air felt, what the colors were, or how the trees and hills appeared at a particular moment. I can relate almost every single word that Catie and I spoke that day, and after all these years, I can picture her perfectly. But except for what we talked about, I can't remember anything else about that part of the walk across the valley from Hebronetta's. Catie and I might as well been far up in the sky floating with the vapors of clouds. The rest of the world was nothing. She was real and she was the only thing that existed.

"Catie, when did you first see me?"

"Remember the day you came to the house? When the moving van was there?"

"Uh huh."

"Well, I remember that all of a sudden I was just sitting in that seat on the front porch, watching you get out of the car."

"What do you mean 'all of a sudden'?"

"I don't remember anything before that except lying in a hospital bed with my mother and father beside me."

"You mean you haven't been wandering around here since 1938?"

"If I have, I don't remember it."

"What do you remember about the day you, uh . . ."

"You can go ahead and say it. The day I died. I get sad about it, but it happened, and there's nothing I can do to change it. Anyway, I had been real sick. I had some kind of fever, and everything was cloudy and dream-like. I remember waking up and seeing my parents. I could see everything so clearly. I could hear well, and I could think well. Mama and Daddy had been crying, so I asked them if I was going to die, and they said certainly not. But I sensed that wasn't true. Daddy turned around to cry, and I knew he wouldn't have done that if everything had been all right. I told them I knew I was going to die, and I didn't mind talking about it. Even though they never really admitted I was going to die, we talked about death. I told them I had one wish and one regret. The wish was that I wouldn't be forgot-ten. The regret was that I had never had a boyfriend. My parents said they would never forget me, but I knew that after they went, there would be no one to remember me."

"But Catie," I protested. "That's the way with every-one sooner or later. Even if you have children and grandchildren, somewhere down the line, in some gen-eration, you'll be forgotten. I don't know anything about my great-great-great grandparents. It may be sad, but it happens to all of us."

"Yes, I guess so. I never thought of it that way," she said, lowering her head, then raising it with a smile. "That makes me feel better." We were silent for awhile. Catie, I could tell, was deep in thought, then she said, "You know, Billy, I remember when I was a little girl, five or six years old, we went to my great grandfather's funeral. On the way home, my daddy bought me a balloon, you know, one of those helium-filled ones. About a mile from our house, he stopped the car, and we got out. He took my balloon and let it go. It went way up, and we followed it with our eyes 'til it disappeared. My dad said death was like that. We're like a balloon that rises to heaven."

"Do you remember anything that happened after you died?"

"Not right now, but I think there have been times during the last few months that I have remembered. It's just so unclear now. But I do remember smiling at Mama and Daddy. It was because I was thinking about that balloon."

"Do you remember what Hebronetta told me?" I asked.

"About what?"

"About why, uh, ghosts come back?"

"No. What?"

"She said they come back to get something they missed out on. I'll bet you came back to have a boy-friend. And," I said grinning, "here I am."

Catie laughed, pushed me away, then snuggled up next to me after kissing me on the cheek. Her hair smelled so good. I hugged her for a long time, then we held hands and stepped back from each other. She said, "I started liking you the first time I saw you. You stood there near the road and stared. It was like you were looking straight into my eyes."

"That's strange. I thought the house was staring at me. I remember getting such a funny sensation."

"Well, as you say, that was Catie Waldrop hunting for a boyfriend. I used to watch you all the time. I would hide from you, 'cause I didn't want you to see me. After I'd spied on you awhile, I really began to like you. A lot. But I was always afraid you wouldn't like me."

"Just like people worry about in real life," I said.

"Just like in real life," said Catie.

"Then you started going out with me."

"Uh huh. And I was scared you were going to have a date with Susan Morrison. I really got jealous."

We reached our destination and stayed only a few minutes before turning back toward the point where we had met that morning. The day was heading toward late afternoon. We walked awhile in silence. Suddenly, I had a pang of melancholy. I brushed it aside and kidded with Catie, but it crept back into me, from head to toe. I looked at Catie. She had a worried look, too.

"Catie, why did we start walking back this way without even deciding to?"

"I wondered that myself. . . . Billy, I feel scared."

"Me, too."

"Let's talk about something else."

"Okay," I said.

I put my arm around Catie's shoulders and pulled her closer. It was a few moments before either of us spoke. She broke the silence and with a smile that pushed aside her worried look, she said "I had a lot of fun that night we went to the drive-in."

"I'll bet you did. I can't believe I sat in the front seat while Gary and Paula were in the back seat. I was afraid to move."

"You were really funny. Sitting straight up in the seat. I don't think you moved your head for two hours."

"What did you do all that time?"

"I turned around and watched them all through the show."

I laughed. Catie laughed. The first soft winds of the north hit us, blowing Catie's long hair. I told her her hair was pretty. She brushed it aside and said thank you.

"Do you all always go to the drive-ins like you did that night?" She was referring to Gary and Paula getting in the trunk of the car a block or so from the theater. That way, I would only have to pay for one admission, then they would each give me one-third of the price.

"As much as we can. It sure saves some money."

Catie pointed toward the creek. "Billy, look. The creek is rising. We had better get across. I've seen it really get high. I can remember once when it went a half mile out of its banks. A lot of cattle and horses were killed."

We did get wet, but the crossing was not difficult. In those drought years, it would be a long time before we saw any high water.

When we got to the other side, Catie became quiet again. As we walked, she laid her head on my shoulder and said nothing. We reached the ridge and sat down, not concerned about the wet grass. The creek bottom spread out below us. It seemed as if the shower had added more green to the trees in a few short hours. The sky was clear except for a small layer of clouds that seemed to be hovering, almost motionless, west of where we sat, and a few remnants of clouds that remained far off to the east. The sun had speeded up and was getting close to the edge. It reflected off the layer of clouds and gave a gold tint to the valley in front of us. I gazed at Catie. She was golden, even the freckles across her nose and under her eyes. I was as happy as I had ever been and as sad as I had ever been. All in the same body. All at the same time. I could see the same paradox in Catie's face.

"Billy, this is all so unbelievable. I don't think it's going to last."

"I don't want you to go."

"I don't want to."

"Let's walk," I said. We rose, stretched and looked sadly at each other. The high point was only a few yards ahead of us.

"Billy, I've had a wonderful time. Not just today, but for the last year. No one could have any better memories than I have."

"I have too, Catie. But tomorrow'll be even better. We can go to some different places, like into town."

She said nothing. Her eyes filled with tears, and one slid down her cheek, followed by others. I kissed her.

"I love you, Catie."

Catie looked up at me and said, "Billy, would you promise me something?"

"Sure."

"Promise me you'll never forget me."

"I promise, Catie."

She wiped her tears, but they kept coming. She turned and walked away from me.

"Catie?" I heard her sniffing. "Catie?"

Her hand brushed her eyes as she turned toward me. With her finger tips, she rubbed the tears beneath her eyes, then smiled at me and laughed a little.

"Billy, do you remember that night down at Burgers and Cream?"

"The first time you and I went out?"

"Yeah," she grinned mischeviously as she spoke. "Well, you know those Cokes and french fries? They. . . ."

Catie vanished.

"Catie?" I whispered.

"Catie!" I screamed.

It was silent except for a meadowlark singing behind where Catie had stood. I turned slowly and looked in every direction. There was no trace of her. When I headed for home, the sun was slipping downward over the horizon, and it was red, a sign of coming dust. I put my right arm to my nose. I could smell Catie's perfume. The perfume I had given her for Christmas.

If a love letter isn't received, it doesn't have much meaning. I guess that's why I can't remember what I wrote to Catie the night of the day I spent with her. I do remember locking the door to my room to keep Beth out and sitting at my desk late at night, alternately writing the letter and staring at the pictures of Catie that I had propped up on my desk against the wall.

The clock said almost midnight when I finished writing. I took the letter with me to the bois d'arc tree where I left it beside a flower I had picked in Mother's garden on the way out of the house.

When I got back from the tree, I easily went to sleep with images of Catie and me walking together, but a couple hours later, I awoke, wide awake. I don't remember whether I had ever thought about the terms, "heavy heart," "heartache," "aching heart," or such. "Depression" was not a word much in vogue among teenagers in those days, but I experienced all those states that night.

When I awoke, my heart was all the way back to my backbone, hurting and trying to sink through the bed, the floor, and into the ground. That was the first time I actually realized that I might not see Catie again, and there was nothing I could do to repel the thought. At one time during the long night, I got out of bed and slipped out to the tree. The wilted flower and my letter were still there, but I rationalized by telling myself that Catie probably came early in the morning. It didn't help. I got back in bed and sank even lower, my low feelings increased by the knowledge that there would be no one to whom I could tell my problem.

Just after sunrise, the letter was lying right where I had left it. There was no sign that Catie had come to the tree. As I walked home, my eyes burned from lack of sleep, and my spirits sank lower and lower. The morning moon, a day past its fullness, hung in the west, but it no longer affected me. Doves, softly calling to each other, had no meaning as they had at other times.

The following days seemed to be without end. I fell into a deep depression, without the consolation of friends. I had never before felt so alone. School went on and on and on. The weekend was rainy, and staying inside and watching the darkness caused my spirits to fall even farther.

I continued writing notes to Catie and religiously continued to place them in the tree. Nights, I wandered over the hills and along the creek looking for her. Sometimes I would sob a little, and sometimes I would call out her name. Once, down by the rock, I yelled, "Catie" over and over, but was answered only by a weak echo.

Beth noticed my mood and asked me several times what was wrong. She tried to be nice to me, but I turned her away. My parents also noticed my change, but for several days, they said nothing. Often, though, I caught Mother staring at me when she thought I wasn't looking. One time, she asked me if everything was all right. I said yes.

Mother did not accept that answer. On a weekend afternoon in late April, she called me into the kitchen where she and Dad were standing. She asked me to sit down, then she told me that she and Dad did not mean to pry into my affairs. Dad said they had a good idea what my problem was, and they weren't going to ask me any questions, but they did want me to listen to what they had to say.

My parents did know the problem, but of course they didn't know who the girl was. They took turns telling me that in real life, things don't always work out the way we want them to work out, that both of them had had heartbreaks, that they realized that telling me they had gone through the same experiences would not pull me out of the depths, but at least it would help to know that you can survive. Dad finished by saying, "The only way to avoid being hurt is to never take a chance, but life isn't worth living if chances are not taken. Billy, you never would have had your wonderful basketball experience if you had not tried out for the team. Remember, most of the year you failed, but the one time you succeeded far overshadowed the times you did so poorly."

I thought to myself that I didn't even do that. Catie did.

Dad continued, "You have a way of being interested in the things around you, of trying to do things, of trying to stretch out just a bit farther than you can go. Hemingway's character in *The Old Man and the Sea* said that he didn't fail, he just went out too far. And I know it hurts when you go out too far. You didn't fail. You just sought the wrong thing. And it won't be the last time things like this happen. But there will be many other times when things will be better."

Mother said, "You don't have to comment, Billy. Why don't you just take a long walk and see if that helps." They left the room, and I sat at the kitchen table, alone.

My thoughts were jumbled. Most of all I wanted to find Catie, but I also wanted to break out of the doldrums I was in. I didn't admit to my parents that I thought they were right, but I must have allowed their advice to slip by the barriers that were being created by my growing up and breaking away. A few minutes after they had left the room, I walked out to the hills toward the creek, thinking about what they had said, but telling myself it was mainly to search for Catie.

For the first time since she had disappeared, I was able to see the things around me, not as I used to see them, but at least better than I had for two weeks. I looked at the bois d'arc tree, standing all alone on the prairie. I saw its broken places, scars of where old limbs had once been, almost leafless limbs that wouldn't hold up to too many more winds and winters. Before long, I thought, I would pass that spot, and the tree would not be there. It would exist only in the collage in my head. Like Dallas. . . . Like Catie. That thought sent me reeling again.

Farther out in the pasture, I began the gentle ascent that led to the high point above the creek. The hills were rolling in green and all of the other colors of spring. The rain, following a long dry period, had brought out more flowers than I had ever seen.

Near the high point, I sat down. To my left were the tops of the tall cottonwoods that grew along the creek. Beneath me, the hill sloped gradually downward, then rose again on the other side of the trough. I sat at that point for an hour or so, letting my thoughts go which-ever way they wanted. They never went far from Catie. The ache remained.

I must have dozed. My head was on my arms, which were resting on my knees. I looked around at the creek and decided to go back to the house instead of down to the water. I stood up and blinked, adjusting my eyes to the light, then slowly moved back toward home.

A shrill whistle sounded high above me in the direc-tion of the house. I shaded my eyes and spotted a hawk. I watched it fly east, then west, then directly at me as it screeched again. The hawk pulled up and slowly climbed toward the east before turning north and flying just above the ground on the ridge that paralleled the ridge on which I was standing. It turned once more toward me as if it were trying to get my attention. I watched it fly in low, wide circles above the opposite hill and listened to it screech again and again.

My eyes must have been focused directly on the hawk, because it was several seconds before I noticed the hillside beneath the bird. What I saw caused me to instantly forget the hawk. I stepped back. My eyes got wider. I know that I smiled, and for sure, I choked up. The opposite hillside was almost solid spring green, a perfect carpet. Within the green were masses of pink primrose. They spelled out the words:

"Catie loves Billy."

I sat down. I cried a little. I laughed a little. I went across and walked among the primroses, then came back and gazed at the words until dark. My head had cleared, and the ache was gone, although I knew a little hurt would always remain. I had experienced finality, and I knew I would survive. As the flowers disappeared in the twilight, I turned and headed toward home. And toward summer. And toward the rest of my life.

I never saw Catie Waldrop again.

Afterword

1992 I'm surprised how little the countryside has changed in thirty-six years. A few new houses have appeared in the intervening time, and Oakpoint has moved northward quite a ways, but mostly everything looks the same now as it did then. And early May in 1992 is just as lovely as spring was in 1956.

While I was in college, my parents moved from the country, so I seldom come back to visit the old home. Today is the first time I've returned in probably twenty years.

As we drive north on the state highway, my wife Molly is the only one, besides me, looking at the passing countryside and listening to my rambling stories of what happened at this place and that place. Molly and I have three children, two boys and a younger girl. They're in the back seat, but they can't hear anything, because they are wearing headsets. I have a theory that headsets not only eliminate conversation, but they also blind the kids. It's as if their ears are connected to their eyes in such a way that if the volume is loud enough, their optic nerves are disconnected, and they lose all sensual contact with the outside world. At least they're quiet, though, and there's no badgering and fighting, only some periodic bouncing up and down with the beat of the music.

Earlier this morning, I took the family to some of my old haunts in Oakpoint. The first visit was to my junior high. I had built it up with many stories and was disappointed when we discovered it had been torn down and a new building constructed in its place. The kids reacted with a simultaneous rolling of the head and eyes. We drove by Central Junior High. Except for the old gymnasium, it was gone, too. Davy Crockett Elementary had been imploded only a month before our visit, and B&C was a bar. Man-made landmarks are permanent only to one generation. The next generation's buildings will be the ones that took the place of ours, and my children will mourn when those are demolished. Then maybe they will remember that their dad had some places sacred to him.

Thank goodness the road to our old house has not changed. It's still graveled, and that's comforting. Johnson grass still grows tall along the edges and leans out into the road like it's welcoming me back. Before we left town, I called the present owners of the land and obtained their permission to walk around the property. I had no interest in seeing the inside of the house particularly since siding had been placed on it. With new occupants, it would no longer be my house, and my attachments are with the never-changing, not the renovated. The creek and the hills mean a lot more to me than the house.

I park the car about where my dad first parked his car and point in the direction we'll be walking. The children jump out and sprint ahead of Molly and me, and I start to yell at them to come back, but think better of it. They can enjoy roaming more if they don't have to listen to my reminiscing.

We leave the house and outbuildings behind and walk past the spot where the bois d'arc once stood. It is now bald prairie covered only by a variety of grasses and yellow coreopsis that continually move back and forth in response to the waxing and waning of the south wind. A few mesquite trees are also scattered in the pasture, a sign of poor land management. I don't know what feelings to expect when I take this walk through so many memories, but so far it's only a pleasant stroll through rolling plains, flowers, grass, and sky. Lots of sky. I'm trying to let some of the old emotions work their way back in, but can't force a feeling. At the top of the ridge, I yell at the kids and make a pointing motion toward the creek. They understand and run down the hill full speed. Molly turns her head to avoid witnessing what she anticipates will be our daughter's inevitable fall. She makes it, though, only a few feet behind the boys, and they all disappear into the foliage. When Molly and I reach the creek, the kids are on a sandbar, dipping their shoeless, sockless feet into the water. I tell them we're lucky it has been several days since the rains came. Otherwise, crossing would be impossible.

All of them want to go to Hebronetta's place. I've told them so many stories about her that she has reached mythical proportions. I tell the kids, "Okay, but before you go to Hebronetta's, you have to give the same signal I gave when I went there. See that big oak over there? Everyone meet me at its trunk."

They splash through the shallow water and race to touch the tree first. I say, "Now climb up on that large limb and 'hoot' three times like an owl."

They do. I wait, almost expecting Kern and Tipps to show up. They don't, of course, so the five of us begin jogging up what was once a pretty good trail but now is used only by an occasional fisherman. When we reach the little valley, I point out where the cabin once stood. Very little evidence of it is left. I can see tombstones at the graves, so I call the kids and tell them to come look where Hebronetta is buried. When we get there, I see Mr. Isbell kept his promise, but I'm momentarily puzzled, because there are three monuments instead of two. I read the inscriptions silently.

Homer Winslow Sikes
Born ?? Died 1943
"A good husband and a good father"

Homer Winslow Sikes Jr.
Born 1900 Died 1918
Brought back home 1961

Hebronetta Magdaline Sikes
Born 1881 Died 1956
Gone? Maybe.

My eyes begin to tear up. So do Molly's, because I've told her about Hebronetta and her son, and she has always thought that was such a sad story. She shakes her head and looks at me with a smile in her eyes.

"She must have been something, Billy."

"She was something, really something," I say. A wisp of how I felt long ago blows by me, and I catch a little bit of it.

Molly says, "It's nice how someone's kept up these graves."

"Yeah, it is," I answer. "I wonder who does it since the Isbells died."

Mark, our oldest, brings some flowers over and sets them on Hebronetta's grave. I tell him the red and yellow flower is an Indian paintbrush. The little white flowers with the yellow centers, the ones that look like daisies, are fleabane. For a split second, I'm again transported back and the feelings of that day with Catie engulf me. Catie is handing me the flowers. Then, she and the feeling disappear.

We have to catch a plane in about three hours, Molly reminds me, so I call the kids and tell them it's time to go. They want to stay and say so in the stalling, defiant manner of children, but after promises that we'll come back some time soon, they reluctantly agree to leave the little valley. As usual, they dart ahead, leaving Molly and me alone with only the sound of a few birds and the children's voices fading fast as they outdistance us. The lush green tops of the cottonwoods sway high above us.

For a while, the two of us walk in silence. More of the old memories start creeping back. It's like they are attacking in little waves, then backing off. I look around, expecting to see Hebronetta. I even wonder if Catie is watching us. I don't try to figure out anything that happened back then. I gave up on that a long time ago.

Catie came back seventeen years after her death. She was still fourteen. So was I. Now I'm a month away from fifty-one. A Robert Louis Stevenson poem about the death of a young person, one I memorized years ago, comes back to me.

> Yet, O stricken heart, remember, O remember
>   How of human days he lived the better part.
> April came to bloom and never dim December
>   Breathed its killing chills upon the head
>   and heart.
>
> Doomed to know not Winter, only Spring, a being
>   Trod the flowery April blithely for a while
> Took his feel of music, joy of thought and seeing
>   Came and stayed and went, nor ever ceased to
>   smile. . . .

It's a beautiful rationalization and a wonderful attempt at giving comfort, but I feel a tinge of sadness thinking of all the things, both good and not so good, that Catie missed. Dim Decembers and winters make brighter Aprils. Again the feeling of youthful love and infatuation I had for Catie zips in and out of my head, just long enough for me to recapture it. Then it's gone.

No one, not even me, can realize what effect knowing Catie had on me. Throughout my adult life, I have read about and listened to speculations of an afterlife and what happens. There have been hundreds of books written about ghosts, some of them serious, some of them just fun. I had thought about telling of my expe-

rience at a dinner party. Just right out of the blue.
Nobody would have believed me, though. I know that.
And if I had continued to tell it, trying to be convincing,
everyone would begin to think I'm crazy. I'm not pre-
occupied with this story, because I have too many other
interests and responsibilities. But I always knew I would
have to tell it sometime. Otherwise Catie would have
been forgotten, and that would be a breaking of my
promise. Whatever else happens, I don't want her forgotten. When I wrote the story I changed all the names
except hers. I used another name for my home town. It
was easy to switch the other names around and do things
like change the make up of my family and its history.
But I didn't change Catie's name . . . or Hebronetta's.
Maybe someone will do enough research and find that
they did really exist.

Molly, who likes to walk and think as much as I,
breaks the silence. "Billy, if you had the chance, would
you go back?"

"In a New York minute, I would," I say.

"So would I. . . . Do you remember your first
girlfriend?"

"Certainly."

"What was her name?"

"Catie Waldrop."

Molly laughs then says, "I can't believe you never
told me that."

"We all have to have a few secrets."

"My first boyfriend was Joel McCray."

"The movie star?"

"No, just a kid that lived up the block."

"And I bet you liked him."

"A lot. . . . I couldn't think of anything or anyone else. . . . You know, I was thinking about him, and some others, earlier while we were walking. When you talk about relationships, history is so important."

"What does that mean?"

"Well, you can't compare your first love with a twenty-year marriage. There was that wonderful infatuation, but no history, nothing to fall back on. You and I have children, and Lord knows that's an experience. We have our dating days, our first year of marriage. Being broke all the time . . . and surviving. Think of all the trips we've taken. And illnesses. Even pretty strong arguments. I would have a hard time leaving all that history. It's too much a part of me. And you."

"So you've just convinced yourself you wouldn't go back?"

"I guess so. And, who knows, if we went back, we might take a different route and not ever meet each other."

"I sure wouldn't like that," I say and reach over to kiss her.

"Me either."

The kids are on a ridge opposite us. The boys have run to the top, and whatever they're doing, it involves chasing and hitting and lots of noise. Their sister is down the hill from them, picking flowers. She always does a lot of that.

Molly and I stand, holding hands, watching them. Our daughter runs down her hill then up ours and greets us, all smiles, with a bouquet of wildflowers in each hand. She hands a bunch to each of us and says, "I love you."

Molly and I reply, "We love you, too, Catie."

The boys are running ahead. Molly says she and Catie will go on, so I can have one last look by myself. Before I leave, I turn and look down to the creek and across the valley. It's just like it always was.

Above me the morning clouds have been replaced by summer cumulus which have been steadily entering the sky from the southwest. I watch them drift across like the people who drifted across my life while I lived at this place. Gary, the Isbells, Earnie, Hebronetta, Coach Chambers, Wanton. And most of all Catie. I hope my childhood theory of clouds being spirits is true. Maybe Catie has come in to see me. Looking up, I smile, just in case. I want to believe the smile is returned.

I hear a high, far-off screech. I look up and see a hawk flying high to my right. It coasts, then flaps its wings and every so often appears to be looking at me. It swoops and when it reaches the creek, it flies up-stream, skimming the treetops. I watch until it disap-pears.

"Daddy," I hear Catie calling.

"What?" I answer loudly.

She yells, "Mother says there's no moon tonight. The big star will pass over."

"I know," I reply.

Catie says something I can't understand.

I put my hand to my ears and yell, "I can't hear you."

She yells back, "And everything will be all right?"

I cup my hands around my mouth and answer against the south wind, "Yes, it will, Catie. Everything will be all right."